CTHULHUSATTVA

TALES OF THE
BLACK GNOSIS

edited by
SCOTT R JONES

Martian Migraine Press
electronic edition 2016

CTHULHUSATTVA
Tales of the Black Gnosis

edited by Scott R Jones

Ruthanna Emrys' *The Litany of Earth* made its first appearance
on Tor.com, May 14, 2014

Cover illustration
XV. The Devil
© 2015 Alix Branwyn
Interior illustrations
© 2016 Michael Lee Macdonald

National Library of Canada Cataloguing in Publication Data

ISBN (ebook) 978-1-927673-17-1
ISBN (print) 978-1-927673-16-4

martianmigrainepress.com

CONTENTS

CORRELATING the CONTENTS

At some point (don't ask me when it was, exactly, or what triggered the change) I just got tired. A profound enervation settled upon me, dank and heavy and dull. I mean, I had been at the game a while. Not as long as the Joshis or the Prices and the rest for whom the old-school colours of a Miskatonic U tie still hold heart-stirring meaning, mind you, but *still*, long enough. So, perhaps it was to be expected, this weariness. In the bones. A cloying, slightly greasy fog of exhaustion that clogged my frontal lobes whenever the Name was mentioned...

Yes, I was tired of Lovecraft.

And unlike, say, London, when one is tired of Lovecraft one is *not* tired of life. Not really. You're not even tired of weird fiction. Or horror. Or even (dare I say it?) the Cthulhu Mythos. For there is still great, interesting, and engaging work being done within those (admittedly arbitrary) borders. Always has been, and, Dagon willing, always will be. No, what I was tired of was the myth of Lovecraft. The man, the hero (to some), the apparent exemplar of all the things a writer of the weird should be, the letters (god, the letters, the *volumes* of correspondence!), the same three photographic portraits of the Old Gentleman used as guide for every piece of art you could find with him as the subject. It was all too much of a muchness.

Upon reflection, though, it wasn't even Lovecraft the man so much that wearied me. When I started reading "Cthulhu stuff" back in the early 90s, there was a good deal of loving pastiche about, sure. As the years wore on, though, as the man and his Mythos took on bulk and spread into the wider public consciousness, that pastiche became endemic, and (it seemed to me) much of the love that informed it in early days had been lost. There was a formula, you see. Beats to hit. Names (of books, places, people, *things*) to check. A style sheet. Some employed it well. Others, not so much.

What was missing? The thrill was gone, certainly. The flavour, lost. Ashes, ashes... but *something* had burned there. I took a break (needs must!) and then, resolute, I returned to the stories for a deep reading. Not a scholarly examination (scholarship just ain't my bag, and I leave it in the capable hands of the aforementioned MU alumni) or even a literary one. This was a deep reading to plumb the *soul* of the Mythos, to trace the glowing lineaments of its spirit, to find the strangely-angled stone beating like a monstrous heart (slowly, slowly, with the patient pulse of long aeons) at the centre of my connection to Lovecraft.

It was a search not without its inherent treacheries. For every gem I unearthed in my reading, there was often an attendant shrill piping from the imaginary Lovecraftian peanut gallery in my head. When Cthulhu rises from the waves in the final act of the titular tale, I would feel the stirrings of a potent religious terror. *A mountain walked or stumbled.* But from the gallery: "Not a god! Lovecraft was an atheist! Alien monstrosity from beyond the stars, but not a god!" Oh, fine. Have it your way. When Peaslee feverishly narrates the revelations of his Yithian psychic kidnapping, and vast cosmic vistas yawn wide on the page, I would feel a species of awed contentment at the thought that consciousness is fluid and evolving and that, in an infinite universe, something would always survive. The gallery: "It's horrific! Existence is meaningless, man is doomed! Beetles will rule the Earth!" Well, thanks for killing the beautiful transhumanist buzz I had going there, fellas. And when Robert Olmstead breaks his mutating cousin out from a mental institution and, with his brand spanking new vestigial gills sucking at the moisture in the New England night air, vows to make his way to Devil Reef in order to accept his Deep One heritage (genetic *and* cultural, I should take pains to point out), I was right there with him thinking "wonder... glory... forever". Shrieks from the gallery, though: "He's tainted! *Tainted!* Insane! Oh, monstrous miscegenation! Oh, hideous fate!" And so on.

Please. Enough with your taint. (Also, *eww.*) Enough with the fear, primal or otherwise. As for the nihilism, well, sounds to me like it needs to get out for a bit of air under the stars. Maybe watch the black planets roll without aim for a while. Keep its mouth shut, and let it all soak in.

Because, at the end of that deep read, I realized that the things in Lovecraft that spoke to me (and, I hope, to *you*, dear reader) were these: Awe. A species of spiritual terror that bordered on enlightenment. Transcendence. Deep, cosmic mystery. And knowledge. With a capital K. Or, as the Greeks liked to call it, Gnosis.

I won't burden you with what came after this minor literary epiphany. You can always read my auto-ethnographical work *When the Stars Are Right: Towards An Authentic R'lyehian Spirituality* if you feel like some non-fiction fun and are curious to see what can be built from the genuinely weird religious stuff found between Lovecraft's lines. For now, though, here in this place and this time, I want to speak to that experience, that Gnosis (and while we're at it, let's throw an appropriate colour on it and call it *the Black Gnosis*), and about the anthology you hold in your hands.

In *Cthulhusattva: Tales of the Black Gnosis*, you will find no dry tales of finely-tuned nervous college types getting on the wrong side of a nasty old book from the special collections. (I lie, a little: the narrator of Vrai Kaiser's *Keys in Stranger Deserts* starts there, but quickly moves off campus, and she's no nervous wreck.) Neither are there stories here of your standard Lovecraftian cultist: robes and ceremonial daggers are left at the door, as is that very particular crazed mindlessness we're so used to. (Don't worry, there's still a chant here and there.) And the gods (yes, *gods*, put that in your trilby and smoke it, peanut gallery!), the Great Old Ones themselves, are perhaps more awe-inspiring than ferocious within these pages. But then, as any spiritual seeker knows, deities tend to reflect back upon a supplicant the qualities they already carry to the altar. And the seekers herein are (for the most part) open, thoughtful, willing, and broad-minded. They are ready for the deadly light of revelation. They welcome it, and for one reason alone...

It is still *light*.

A mother and daughter carry out Nyarlathotep's divine will with reason and humility in the face of ignorant mania in John Linwood Grant's *Messages*, while two sisters move far beyond their comfortable worlds to hear the final shattering revelation of their curiously long-lived grandfather in Luke Maynard's *That Most Foreign of Veils*. In *Antinomia*, by Erica Ruppert, we travel with an unlucky medium and her followers across an apocalyptic landscape toward a meeting with destiny. Love, desire, and the power of lust are stripped back to their bare essences in Kristi DeMeester's heartbreaking *The Wicked Shall Come Upon Him* and the heady robustness of Gord Sellar's *Hieros Gamos*, while the temporary and ephemeral nature of the flesh is explored in Rhoads Brazos' *Feeding the Abyss* and Stefanie Elrick's excellently Barker-esque *Mother's Nature*.

There are sorcerers here, some wise (Don Raymond's dark nativity play *We Three Kings*) and some less so, though not for lack of trying (the wūshī who brings upon himself a grisly immortality in *Emperor Eternal* by Konstantine Paradias), and others for whom magic is a tool to be respected, like the famous Mississippi blues man called to the crossroads to combat the arrogant strivings of a struggling pulp horror writer in Jamie Mason's *Mr. Johnson and the Old Ones*. Jayaprakash Satyamurthy reveals the true nature of those Old Ones, and their ultimate expression, as deduced by those who wait *At the Left Hand of Nothing*.

Which brings us to the feature novella, Ruthanna Emrys' *The Litany of Earth*. This story first saw publication on Tor.com, and has appeared elsewhere since then, but I believe *Litany* has found its true spiritual home here in the humble pages of *Cthulhusattva*. This is something I feel confident in saying, and I'm grateful to Ruthanna for working with me so graciously to place it here. When I first read *Litany*, I knew it immediately for what it was: a perfect jewel of a story, each facet shedding light on some aspect of the Mythos that spoke to me. There is awe here, wonder and glory. There is pain that transforms, and longing, and compassion in the face of unknowable forces in an uncaring universe. In Aphra Marsh, Emrys has given us a character unlike any Lovecraftian protagonist that has gone before: wise, passionate, possessed not only of the strength of her physical heritage, but also that of her culture and history. If this is your first meeting with Ms Marsh, then I am happy it is here, and I envy you the experience.

Listen. Sunken bells toll in the deep. The stars sing of a death that is not death as they turn in their velvet sockets. Sleepers beneath the earth, and in the space between spaces, murmur of strange awakenings; do not mistake that sound for mere wind. Within your chest, between the beats of your mortal heart, the non-Euclidean towers and migraine cathedrals of the First City, the Dreaming City, begin to rise, and there is a burnt ozone taste of eternity in the air. Breathe. Centre yourself. And open your mind to the cosmos. For you are now invited to take the Cthulhusattva Vow, and learn that which only the enlightened can truly know...

When all is madness, there is no madness.

Scott R Jones
2 March 2016
Victoria, BC

CTHULHUSATTVA: TALES OF THE BLACK GNOSIS

6

The PEARL in the SHADOWS

Bryan Thao Worra

"When the sage points at R'lyeh, the madman stares at the tentacle."

Once you understand the truths of a centerless cosmos,
Know you will be condemned to return in a thousand forms.

Some will pipe and some will scream,
Some will whisper and crawl.
A few for the right reasons.

Some will write a poem with something shaped like a man
On a filthy morning filled with the laughter of the finite.

Some will find wisdom like a Valusian serpent in Leng,
Others will remain fools, dreaming of their roots in Vientiane
Or the questionable tastiness of a Miskatonic mudbug.

Those who dare to hope will fall asleep many times,
Those who dare to wake will see something timeless.

Yawp as you will among sacred worms and stumbling mountains.
Though you are but one grain in the multiverse,
In our darkness, what a pearl you might yet become.

Know your true name is already a scrawl in the Book of the Dead,
Your ultimate fate as certain as a well-read poet in a nameless bazaar
Remembered and sought only for their most nonsensical scribbles.

WE THREE KINGS

Don Raymond

THE STARS WERE RIGHT.

It hung in the west, in the sign of the fish: the searing gaze of a newborn god; and the skies were mad with lights. Rising in the constellation Pisces, the planets touched, merged, and burned as one.

They read the scrolls, ancient when man was young, and they knew what must be done. Their bags were heavy, filled with gold, with frankincense and myrrh, and the iron-bound books they carried: *The Method* of their master—and the other.

It was their final rite. When all the trials were passed, they would climb the hundred thirty-seven steps, to the room with no windows, there to read the book of the mad Arab. Not all who made that journey returned, and not all who returned were the same.

But they had. They were the greatest of their Order, and they carried it with them now, in their time of greatest trial. By night, Balthasar would turn to the prophecy written therein:

"I shall see him, but not now: I shall behold him, but not nigh: There shall come a Star out of Jacob, and a Sceptre shall rise out of Israel..."

Melchior would answer, reading from their own holy book:

"If two lines are drawn which intersect a third in such a way that the sum of the inner angles on one side is less than two right angles, then the two lines inevitably must intersect each other on that side if extended far enough.

"We contradict by construction ..."

They went by secret ways, hiding as much as was possible from the three-lobed burning eye in the heavens. They ate dates, and their beards were long.

As they came up from a wadi, they met four travelers riding eastward.

"Do you seek the new King?" their leader asked.

"We may say only that we travel towards the sunset," Gaspar replied.

The leader drew back his cloak, reaching for his sword. His hands were strangely shaped, and his eyes glowed in the torchlight. "Our lord has warned us of you," he said, as his companions drew their weapons.

But Balthasar drew a Sign, which hung in the air, to freeze them in their tracks. The Magi spurred their mounts forward, leaning low in the saddle, and like silk their blades came forth. There was a brief movement, and the Magi passed through, to cries of *"Iä! Iä!"* from the things that fell behind them, ichor upon the rocks.

They turned again to the West.

For three days they traveled across the waste, keeping Irem to their south. They came upon shepherds abiding in the field, keeping watch over their flocks, though these now fled east, looking back no more. Their hearts were sore afraid, they said; they fled some terrible thing, though they had no name for it. They told the Magi of an old prophecy:

After summer, the winter, and then summer comes no more
From dark seas they shall come crawling
From the wombs of the mothers they shall come crawling ...

And they spoke no more, but turned their faces toward the dawn.

The three travelers watched the lights in the sky, great discs all of shifting colors, that rose and darted across the leering moon. Once, as they lay at rest before their tent, a great beam of light descended from the face of that gibbous orb, to strike in some distant land.

Balthasar muttered from the book of the Mad Arab, *"A door was opened in heaven: and the first voice which I heard was as it were of a trumpet talking with me; which said, Come up hither, and I will shew thee things: Yog-Sothoth is the key to the gate, whereby the spheres meet ..."*

Gaspar moaned in his sleep.

Then it was that they crossed into the hill country. All around them crumbling peaks rose from the battered sands of the desert canyons. They towered vertiginous above them before dropping into salt basins where strangely-shaped mounds littered the desert floor. It was said these were once the inhabitants of forgotten cities, where abominable rites were practiced in the names of gods no longer spoken in that fire-scorched land.

Water, too, lay below them, but it was dead, dead before ever man had come into this place, though the flies in their teeming trillions gave it a screaming, buzzing voice. From the canyon's depths, a great roar echoed, and there was a rushing, of distant wings. They moved quickly from there.

The next night they stood on the crest of a High Place, and the lights of a city burned before them. The mad star, which had followed them all of their travels, lay upon their right. As they watched, a meteor grew bright in the sky, flared, burned through the dark, and was gone.

"The star is a warning," Balthasar said.

His companions looked strangely at him, but said nothing. They roused their mounts, and entered the city.

Torches burned in every room of the palace, though the hour was midnight. They spoke briefly with the guards; were brought before Herod, who was King in that land.

Melchior spoke to him, saying, "Where is the child? We have seen the star from our towers, and have come seeking him."

When Herod heard them, he grew frightened, and summoned the priests and wise men.

"What child is this?" he asked.

"In Bethlehem you shall find Him," the High Priest said. He turned to the Magi. "But it is not a thing to be done lightly. What manner of men are you, to seek him out?"

"We have come from the East," Melchior said. "We have studied the geometries of Archimedes, and watched the sky."

"We are men of knowledge, also," the priest replied. "But the thing that comes ... it is from beyond the spaces we know."

Balthasar moved to a window, where Pisces hung doleful in the sky. "Behold, in the sign of Israel. What are your names for those planets?"

"The first is Jove, whom the Israelites call El."

Balthasar nodded. "And the second?"

"Saturnus, his father. A Titan."

Melchior spoke: "Our Master learned the prophecy, when he was in Egypt:

'And I looked, and behold, there was a great star, which was a crown, and a man bearing a pitcher of water, whose name was I AM He that liveth, and was dead; and, behold, I am alive for evermore. And His habitation is even one with your guarded threshold.'

"Not all our Master wrote was kept in their libraries. He fled into the East, where he learned the secrets of Mithra. We are his priests, and we have waited for this day."

"To stop them. This must not be," Gaspar said.

Herod nodded, grasped their arms. "Take my soldiers."

Gaspar shook his head. "They cannot help us. Guard your city. The worst is yet to come."

They found the babe wrapped in swaddling clothes, lying in a manger.

They drew wide the door, and Gaspar turned away, for the stench was nearly intolerable. The animals bleated in terror, trembling away from the Thing. There was an altar stone, and blood shone in the torchlight, through the flies that gathered there.

Melchior moved within, beheld the scene: the mother, cradling the Abomination in her arms, the inheritor of inbred generations among the hill-folk of Jerusalem. She hissed and clutched the infant tighter to her, gurgling her madness and hate at him.

"You are too late," the man said, moving from the shadows. He was gigantic, skin dark with the blood and forgotten heresies of antique Nubia. Sweat rolled from his brow as he heaved his bulk toward them. "He is come again into the land of Caanan."

Gaspar drew his knife, all silver, etched with the geometries of forbidden spaces.

"Only for a time," he said.

Joseph threw back his head and laughed, a hyena's baying bark. "Iä! Iä!" he chanted. "Dagon p'thglui Iä! R'lyeh ntrw dhwty fhtagn!"

A darkness rose in the corner; the cattle lowed in panic as the angles deepened, curved in upon themselves and took on abyssal depth. From within, a shape began to coalesce, moving from immeasurable depths, past stars dead and planets mad with the things that moved upon them.

Then Melchior stood forth and hung a sign upon the air; time slowed, began to creep. The thing inside crawled on, its motions the passage of eons. Melchior raised his arm once more and moved upon the Sign; within each of its seven lines, he drew two smaller lines, and then two more within them. He murmured under his breath, "s is equal to r times theta. Let the absolute value of s minus delta be..." and the angles across which the gibbering thing moved began to grow smaller. From some distant place there was a wail of horror halted, but soon the light began to pool once more in normal space.

Then it was that Balthasar drove his knife into Melchior's back. Melchior fell with a sighing cough, blood trickling from the corners of his mouth, his eyes staring finally at the man who stood above him, wild of beard, grimacing with madness.

"Iä," Balthasar said. "I have seen the Gate, and what moves through it."

Gaspar turned to him, his blade tracing a deadly arc, but Joseph grappled him from behind, and there was no negating the strength of those arms. Gaspar was lifted on high. He braced his hands against Joseph's arm as it moved toward his neck. There was a crack, as of dried twigs under wet leaves, and Joseph dropped him limp to the stable floor.

Balthasar knelt before the child. Reaching into the bag, he pulled forth the great iron-bound book and offered it to the babe. The child smiled, traced one finger along the cover. His eyes were like a goat's. "Iä," he gurgled, and Balthasar rose.

"Herod will send his men. We must leave this place," he said to Mary.

"We will go into Egypt, to the land of my people," Joseph said. "To the Sea of Reeds. There are those there who can teach him."

A light filled the stable, and Balthasar looked outside. A congregation of shimmering discs hovered in the air before the tent. As he looked upon the sky, the bull that was Taurus reared and pawed at the blackness. Roaring, it plunged its horns into the side of Mithra. The dark of night peeled away, revealing the shapes that lurked behind space, until they were obscured by a blossoming cloud that flowed from that terrible wound. The vapors billowed downward, covering the star that had shown the way to that place.

As Balthasar watched, Mithra began to sink below the horizon.

MESSAGES

John Linwood Grant

THE FIRES AT ALEXANDRIA DID not consume. The aedificium of St Michael's abbey burned, but there was only air to fuel the rage. And the House of Wisdom was empty when the Mongols reached the banks of the Tigris.

I know this, because I have seen what they contained, those great libraries of the past. I have touched the legacy of Al-Ma'mun with these hands, and know that ink alone turned the Tigris black. Not the pigments from books or scrolls, as the histories tell, but ink unused, darkness trapped in carboys of glass, waiting to become knowledge.

Hulagu Khan had his day, but we had our nights, so many nights that the House of Wisdom was emptied of everything of value before the horde crushed the horizon.

Nothing shall be lost.

It is His Will, and His Need.

I tell my daughter these things, so that she can understand how great our labours are, and how servitude will, in the end, be freedom. To explain why we are here, in a cold waste that is not Kadath.

She tightens her coat around her, and shivers. There's a sharp wind from the sea today. She knows that her father is still looking for her, but she is thirteen years old. She understands how to turn from security cameras at the rest stops, how to order coffee and pie without being either too furtive or too open. We have had enough time on our own—two years, seven months and nine days—to make our understanding. A daughter's place is with her mother, and her mother's place is where He commands.

Alaska.

"Will we meet them soon?" she asks.

"Yep." I smile, and stroke her ash-blonde hair. "Soon enough. Are you sure, Kitty? You could sit this one out if you want."

She gives me one of those angry *I'm not a kid* looks.

"His Need," she says, flicking her bus ticket angrily against her leg.

Catherine Elly Mayburn. Kitty.

Sometimes, when I sleep and see His faceless anger, I hope that she will have a few years yet. It isn't my decision, but a mother can hope.

I teach her, every day. Languages mostly, and IT skills, of course. These are not the days of Al-Ma'mun. So much information on a handful of memory sticks, an external drive. A single Mongol soldier could destroy an entire library by treading on it.

"It's coming."

I look up, and see the silver-white bus pulling round the corner. We had stowed on a cheap cruise to Seward, and this would be the last leg of our journey north. Seward to Anchorage direct, paid in cash, no trace of two people passing through.

We snuggle together at the back, but it is warm. The bus smells of air-conditioning, that dry, slightly electrical smell, along with a whiff of bourbon from the old man snoring in the next seat forward.

She sleeps. I open my backpack, and search through documents, falsified papers, ID cards made by one of our own people in Seattle. This month we are Barbara Torstein and her niece Eleanor. I am taking Eleanor—Elly is a useful half-lie—on her first visit to Alaska. Dog-sledding and wildlife cruises, an exciting get-away for a teenager from the city. And who knows? We might be allowed to do those things, eventually.

We will find out after Anchorage.

I lay my head on Kitty's shoulder, and let the rumble of the bus take me far from here, far from anywhere...

The White Pines Lodge is cheap, a sad collection of cabins crumbling at the edge of town. The owner doesn't care who we are or what we do, and the amenities are few. The mattresses are slightly stale, and raccoons, or something else, have clawed the furniture. It's perfect.

"Wait for me."

Kitty pouts, kicking her heels against the bed-frame. Dust flares in the acid sunlight.

"I won't be long, sweetie. You know that."

"*Fine.*" She stretches out and reaches for a book from my pack. A fragment of the *Book of Seven Parts*, in an Aramaic translation from the fifth century. Not bad for a thirteen year old. I feel a flush of pride, and mutter a prayer to Him. Pointless, because He is with me, in me, but I come from a long line of Catholics. Even when you change Gods, habits are hard to break.

This is not the Anchorage of the television dramas, all snow and lumberjacks. High summer has reached the wilderness. Kids play in shorts and T-shirts on the grass, girls wear cotton frocks and laugh at awkward boys. The public library is modern, a set of pleasing curves set on a slight rise. Glass and concrete the colour of pale caramel, a satellite dish gleaming on the roof.

I know where I am going. Stack Fifteen, at fifteen hundred hours. The library is busy, and I am nothing to the seekers and chatterers around me. I find the spot easily.

A man of indeterminate age stands in the shadows. His lightweight suit bulges slightly at the waist.

"Hello," he says.

We need no code, we who serve the Messenger. The man's eyes are the same grey as his suit, but what lies behind them is the focused, exquisite madness of our kind. We are ripe with purpose, with knowledge, a kind of sanity which would bring psychologists to their knees, mewling.

"Did it happen?" I can't stop my eagerness from being apparent.

"Two nights ago." He grins. "A Russian deep-water trawler, supposedly with engine trouble. They used a storm in the Chuckchi to argue their way in, and they're dickering over the cost of new parts."

"The package?"

"Passed on, as we expected. I think..." His grin widens. "I think it's genuine. We have a paper trail from Moscow to Provideniya."

Part of me is still in Seattle, though I've tried to brief myself as much as possible.

"It's the nearest decent Russian port," he says, seeing my hesitation.

I nod.

"And the receivers?"

He sneers.

"Schalck, and McConnell."

We both know those names, and what must be done.

"His Need," says the man. The spittle on his lips and the trembling of his hands make me certain of his loyalties. He is excitement and fear in a single breath.

"I'll see to it." I reassure him.

I gesture that I must go, but it is hard to leave this place. The library fills us both with an almost sexual arousal. Here, the air is thick with information, not only the stacks of printed words but the rapid passage of data as students browse the Internet, as the satellite dish on the roof draws down a world of words and images. I can hear it all, feel it in my crotch. The misspelled memes, the complex dissertations, the chatter of Saturday browsers...

This is His Domain, here, as by the River Tigris.

There we took even the smallest fragments of knowledge, down to the tally of bricks being shipped by the slender, white-sailed dhows. Hulago set his Chinese general Guo Kan to the destruction of the city, but destroyed only buildings and people. We saved that which mattered, just as we saved the last fragmentary copy of Homer's *Margites* from the Imperial Library at Constantinople. Only those who came before me knew that it still existed.

The Mongols were no better than the crusaders. They valued nothing, and missed everything.

Kitty is asleep when I get back to the room. I am only a journey-woman in His name, but I can see the fever in her. She will outreach me, if He permits.

If He permits. It took me many years to accept that side of our service. And then, on a slow June morning in Santa Fe, I saw a drunk slam his pick-up truck into a crowd of girls outside the church of St Agnes. Three dead, twenty injured, some of them maybe scarred for life.

In one moment of blood and twisted metal, I understood. This was what our biblical god allowed, either by will or by negligence. No matter how many masses, confessions and Hail Marys there were, a man could still drink a case of malt and drive his battered Chevrolet into dutiful Catholic children.

In one moment of torn flesh, I gave myself fully to His Need.

I am consoled, as I look down on my beautiful daughter, that if she is taken by the great Messenger, or driven into insanities too deep for consciousness to exist, that there will have been purpose behind the act. Pleasure, even, if it is His Will.

She stirs, smiles up at me. One of her socks is almost off her foot, and her hair is a pale radiance on the pillow, hiding the yellowed stains on the nylon cover.

"Are we doing it, mom?"

"Tonight. They have it in a hotel not far from here. The Grand Anchorage Hotel."

Her grin is like that of the man in the library. I sit next to her and riffle through the pages of my notebook. I know what they say, but it thrills me to see the words again.

A single shipment, from the Russian State Library in Moscow. Totally illegal, naturally, and unnoticed by any authority except my people.

Items from far beneath the archives, from cases thrust next to leaking steam-pipes in the dark. I will have to see one of them with my own eyes before I believe that it still exists.

I read, she reads. We go out briefly to eat fried eggs and waffles at a nondescript diner, two normal people doing normal things. I tell Kitty more about the Fourth Crusade, and the destruction of the Imperial Library. A difficult time for our kind—little more than fifty years later the House of Wisdom was lost. His Need was so great, and we were so few.

We go back to the cabins, wash and prepare ourselves. I look at her.

"I'm ready."

"Me too." Kitty has laced up her heavy leather boots, and has her parka on. The temperature is dropping. Fifteen minutes at most to the Grand Anchorage, timed for when the kitchen staff have gone off duty. Our librarian friend told me everything I needed to know. I have a plan of the hotel, and a swipe card for the kitchen entrance.

Somewhere the card's owner, a sous-chef, lies on his bed and shudders, his mind locked onto a wavelength which may kill him before dawn. If it does, they will call it an aneurysm. The Words of the Messenger are not easy to bear, even when the source is a decayed MP3 coming through drugstore earbuds.

Ten at night now, the sky sparkling dark, so much clearer than Seattle. Kitty names the Old Places as we tread the streets. Names of dread, those stars which have little more than a Hubble reference number for most of humanity.

"Ecthe... Inur... Tso'telemen..." One finger traces its way across the heavens, pausing at each point of light.

"Telemi-en."

"Tso'telemi-en," she corrects herself.

"No life in that system now. None of them would listen to His Words."

"Why not?"

I shrug, though I doubt she sees the movement under my thick coat.

"They had a god to protect them, so they thought. Turned out that he wasn't real. The Messenger is."

"What about their knowledge, their books, their tapes, whatever they used?"

"All safe, Kitty."

"Nothing shall be lost," she says, smiling at me.

She puts her small hand in mine, and we turn into the alleys behind the hotel. Anchorage is low and tree-lined, and even the alleys are wide compared to most cities. Two men lounge by a dumpster, smoking and passing a bottle between them. They eye us as we approach.

"Ladies," says one, swaying on his pins. A straggling beard and missing teeth. The two of them move, not enough to block the way, only enough that we would have to edge past them. Drunken sport, I suppose, since I doubt they would actually attack a woman and a teenage girl.

The stars look down on us, and see nothing of interest.

"New t'town?" asks the other man. His lumberjack coat is too tight over a body which hasn't felled a tree in its life. This one is steadier than his friend, full of tension. He smells of the docks, and diesel fuel.

"We have a message," my daughter replies before I can speak.

"Wha' sort o' message, sweetie?" Straggle-beard lurches slightly closer. She looks to me, and I nod. Thirteen is a good age for your first one. You always remember it.

She lets go my hand and goes towards him.

"Shall I whisper it to you?"

There is a disjointed pause. The men are drunk and curious, but they're not getting the reaction they'd expected.

"We should get t'Molly's, Hank." says the dock-man, uneasy.

"It won't take a second." She smiles brightly, then cranes to whisper in Hank's left ear.

The bearded man jerks, his hands flapping like a puppet's as he takes in what Kitty is saying. The bottle hits the ground, rolls under the dumpster, and she steps back.

"Uh, dear God..." he gasps.

He staggers and leans against the grimy plastic container. He tries to speak, but only vomit comes out, a watery spew that goes over his thin legs and his boots. He sinks to his hands and knees, still bringing up cheap liquor and half-digested burger.

"Oh, and my name isn't *Sweetie*. It's Eleanor." Kitty winks at me.

I take the other man by the arm before he can react, and tell him something about myself, something wonderful. I tell him exactly where the Messenger touches me, what He does when He is with me.

We leave them semi-conscious in the alley. They will live, but they will not speak of tonight again.

"Never try that without me." I need to remind her that she is still a girl.

"But I did it right—"

"Never," I say firmly. I know what it is to be a good mother. I didn't have one. "Kitty, darling, there are men who will take advantage of you, you know, touch you where they shouldn't, suggest things..."

I trail off, looking into her dark eyes. Thirteen years old—almost independent, but so vulnerable as well. I trust her, but I remember a boy under the bleachers, and my tears as he reached under my skirt.

My own mother laughed when I told her, said it was how she'd learned. And then she stubbed out her cigarette on the back of my hand and told me to stop sniveling. I carry that moment, and that burn; I go there every time Kitty pisses me off or makes a mistake.

And I am there for her.

"I get it," she says.

We squeeze hands, and slip quietly to the back of the Grand Anchorage. The swipe card opens up a side-door, lets us into a cramped kitchen lit by a couple of night-lights. Orange-red shadows, the faint gleam of knives and stainless steel cabinets.

I want us to have time to leave Anchorage quietly, so there are to be no dramatics if I can help it. My library friend's plan shows service stairs, and we take those. Using this route we won't be seen by the night-staff on the front doors. We'll avoid other guests, and call on Schalck as calmly as possible.

Concrete walls and steps, stained with long-dried spillages. No windows, only another orange light on each landing. The hotel is five storeys high—Schalck is staying on the top floor, in a suite with a view of the bay.

I met him once, in Portland, at an antiquarian book fair. A collector of rare books, a 'cultist' and so-called mystic.

May Father Dagon and Mother Hydra bless you, he murmured. I tried not to laugh. I would rather bed the moaning drunks we left in the alley than spend time with these minor adherents. They talk of secret blasphemies, and mumble in tongues they barely speak. For them, bulging eyes and a wide-lipped mouth make you special. They don't. They make you part of the ephemera, those things which will be blasted into less than dust when the Messenger comes. Y'ha-nthlei will go the same way as Chicago, Beijing, and Buenos Aires.

I had no interest in him, but he saw me as a fellow cultist and kept trying to talk to me. I wasn't in the mood to argue. I murmured a few appropriate responses and left as soon as I could.

At the time Kitty was being held by her father and my latest court petition had failed. She would be brought up a God-fearing child, her father said. And learn some discipline. I still had the bruises from his last explanation of the way the world was supposed to work. I had some thinking to do.

A week after the book fair I took Jimmy at his word. Kitty and I ran, letting the Messenger guide us. Now my daughter is truly disciplined, out of choice, and she fears a God who is more than Sunday service and a collection plate.

I don't think Jimmy would appreciate the irony.

"This is Schalck's floor," says Kitty, pressing the door-bar down.

"Three of them, remember."

Schalck the collector, his confederate McConnell—and the Russian trawler captain apparently, staying on the same floor. Perhaps they are still dickering over the price.

She puts her head round the frame, checking the corridor.

"All clear, mom."

There are two suites on the top floor, one of them empty. The door to the occupied suite is a cream-painted slab of timber that could do with touching up. There's a fish-eye in it which is a bit high for me. I knock and stand back so that I can be seen.

A long pause, and the door is opened. McConnell. I recognize him from a handful of photographs shown to me some time ago. He has a history with the Boston Police Department, following a number of violent episodes near Newburyport. One book collector died, two others were injured during robberies. Commissions from Schalck, I imagine.

"Whatcha want?"

"I'm here to see Mr Schalck. Tell him Susan Krafton needs to talk to him."

Krafton is who I was in Portland. He frowns and shuts the door. A minute later he is back.

"He says to come in."

I nod. "And this is my daughter, Elly."

Kitty waves at him from the corridor, like a shy teenager. This disarms him. His lips make a poor smile, and he beckons us in.

It is not a large suite. Three doors off a main room, and a picture-window smeared with gull droppings which shows off the bay at night. There's no sign of the Russian. Schalck, almost dainty, lounges on the sofa by the window, a shot-glass in one hand.

We who serve the Messenger do not judge by appearances. Schalck and McConnell are ugly inside, small-minded and self-serving. McConnell even looks the part due to the plastic surgery which has widened his mouth and thickened his lips, homage to his professed belief in Dagon. He is wholly human, without any taint of the reef, which must sting him.

Schalck is slim and in his late fifties. I know more about him. He seeks the usual things—immortality, notoriety, wealth. He has the latter, at least. He stays on the sofa.

"Ms Krafton. And your daughter." A tip of his head to Kitty. "You are here for, well, what purpose?"

"The consignment."

"Ah." He uncrosses slim legs, crosses them again. "I'm afraid that this is a private transaction."

Kitty sits on the arm of the sofa farthest away from him.

"Nothing shall be lost," she says.

Schalck stands up, moving away from her. He still has the glass in his hand.

"I'm afraid that you have become a little too involved in your work, Ms Krafton. I know your interest in... certain books is genuine.

You have a smattering of knowledge, yes. But we are diving deep here, far too deep for you."

He and McConnell exchange sly smiles.

"The Elders left Bligh Reef after the Exxon Valdez oil spill." Kitty's own smile is open, guileless. "Y'ha-ngeeth was abandoned by the end of November 1989. In your dating system, I mean, not theirs. They count differently."

The two men stare at Kitty, then at me.

"That's OK, darling. I think we have other matters to discuss."

"You are... one of us?" says Schalck. He makes a sign with his right hand, a twisting of his fingers in the air. I doubt if he really knows what it means.

"I—we—serve another," I say.

"The Dreamer Himself?" His eyes are wide, re-evaluating my importance.

I am getting tired. At this stage it seems easier to leave him to his delusions.

"Show me the Moscow delivery."

The older man considers this, then nods.

McConnell places a chair against the door, then fetches a large oil-stained crate from one of the rooms. He carries it easily, setting it down between Schalck and myself. No one speaks as Schalck removes the loose lid and reaches inside.

He lifts up a manila folder and shows me the three sheets of paper inside, dark with cramped Cyrillic writing. He does not hold them close enough for me to read.

"The transcript of a broadcast from within the Chernobyl reactor chamber, seventeen days after the site had been completely evacuated. From within the chamber!"

His hand shakes a little as he gives the folder to McConnell. The next item he draws out is a wax cylinder wrapped in cloth. He holds it lightly by the ends, as if it might shatter at any moment.

"This is the sound of the Tunguska event, captured by a naturalist's early recording equipment. It's said that the naturalist himself, Abram Tadovich, died on an isolation ward in the port of Archangel." Schalk's laugh is thin and harsh. "A fitting place for one who saw fire in the sky."

That, too, is passed to the other man, who holds the items with reverence in large, clumsy hands. Schalck digs down into fibrous wool packing and removes a smaller wooden container, a cedarwood box the size of a ream of paper.

"And this," he says triumphantly. "Inside this box are fragments of something you cannot imagine, Ms Krafton."

I can feel them, words that have been hidden for millennia. They flare in my mind, drive shafts of aching light into the darkness of my task, His Need. These 'fragments' are part of the vast network of knowledge which He builds through our work. They were at the Library in Alexandria, but went missing. They never reached the House of Wisdom, though my predecessors had hoped to find them there.

It has been a long trail, and they must not be lost again.

"*The Book of Lost Battles*." I breathe. "The record, in an obscure Hebraic variant, of the coming of the archangel Samael to the coastal cities of Canaan. It tells of the retreat of Oannes under Samael's assault. The archangel of death and madness. The Messenger."

I step forward, on the edge of communion with He who rules me.

"Your small god, your Dagon, your Oannes, driven into the deeps by such truths that even he could not bear them..."

"No," Schalck protests. "That wasn't it. There are boundaries for the powers, agreements—"

"There are no boundaries. Not for He of a Million Forms."

I am half McConnell's bulk, but I push him aside with ease. He scrabbles to keep hold of the Tunguska cylinder, frantic.

"Sergei!" McConnell yells, his fish-lips flapping, but it is too late. I am the Message and the Messenger, and Anchorage is no more than an audience, a poor one at that. The lights flicker, and electricity, which is information and thus His Domain, surges around the hotel, shattering street-lamps. Car alarms blare in the streets below.

The Russian appears at a bedroom door, a pistol in one grimy hand, but I am blessed with His Presence. The knowledge of how to use such a device is torn from the man's mind in an instant, and he stands there, staring at the blued metal thing between his fingers. He drops it.

I look to Kitty, who is crouched by the sofa, a feral excitement on her face. She has never seen me go here before.

"The book," I demand.

Schalck stands on the other side of the crate, *The Book of Lost Battles* between us on the packing case. He tears open his shirt, revealing an intricate piece of gold filigree.

"It is mine, by Dagon's Will!" The urbane collector is panicked now, facing true mysteries. An amusing turn of events for a cultist.

"All knowledge is His," I say, and know this to be true because He is with me.

"I have seen Y'ha-nthlei!" Schalck almost shrieks. "I will be a master of those in the deeps, immortal—"

"You will be nothing, and the better for it. You are a dilettante, a mockery."

And I am laughing, lost in coitus with Him, and I know that I have no face, because I can see the demented terror in their eyes as they stare at me, the saliva which dribbles from McConnell's absurd lips. I am between places, beyond their ability to comprehend. They have nibbled on small secrets, like rats, and now they have seen something which can consume them.

Kitty darts forward and grabs the cedarwood box, her arms tight around it.

"I have it, mom," She is trying to look and not look at me.

I am Al-Ma'mun, collecting the thoughts of the world and venerating them, saving them from the dark, for the Dark. I am a cornerstone in the House of Wisdom. If I am shattered, another will be placed there. Perhaps Kitty, if He wills it, but that isn't mine to say.

McConnell is weeping blood, and the Russian has slumped to his knees, his mind torn open by the sight of me. Schalck reaches out, slips, and falls heavily over the packing case, staring up at me. He grips his toy from the depths as if it will somehow protect him.

In the picture window I see my reflection, a featureless plane between chin and hairline. I am taller than a man, and my skin is midnight black. One of His Million Forms, made flesh in me for these short moments.

Or an insanity of my own. Schalck will never understand that it doesn't matter which. To want what he wants is to remain bound, confined by small imaginings.

I have nothing to imagine when He is with me.

The power lines outside the hotel crackle, and lamps begin to shine again. I am a lover brought to the edge, never quite reaching the abyssal heights of His Desire, but it is enough.

Schalck levers himself up on the crate, almost standing. He looks like Jimmy after one of his binges.

"We... serve the same... the same Gods," he wheezes.

"I serve only the Messenger."

And I do what messengers do. I walk away, carrying words that others must hear. Kitty gathers up the cylinder and the manila folder and follows me.

"Nothing shall be lost," she says, trying to emulate my voice.

In the stairwell I stand and draw in deep, shuddering breaths. I am empty.

"*The Book of Lost Battles.*" Kitty strokes the carved cedarwood. We can hear people shouting now, moving down the corridor beyond the fire-door.

"It is His again," I say.

We move quickly down the service stairs, through the kitchen and into the Alaskan night. The two drunks have gone, though the stench of their vomit remains.

I can hear sirens in the vicinity of the Grand Hotel. The three men we have left behind will make no sense. What would they say, even if they could speak? That a small, nondescript woman and a thirteen year old walked unarmed into their suite and robbed them of smuggled artifacts? Ludicrous.

But we leave, because there is work yet to do, in other places.

She is quiet on the way back.

"What will He do with it?" she asks when we are in the shadow of the cabins.

"He will hold it for His Need."

I start laughing again, human laughter this time, and Kitty giggles with me as we let ourselves into our shabby room.

I plug in the electric kettle. Coffee would be good right now.

"He will hold it for the day when He possesses every message that has ever been sent, every message that ever will be sent or left for others. The knowledge, the information of a thousand worlds and a thousand eras."

We sit side by side on the bed, sipping our coffee. She knows much of our people's truths, but I am still burning from the night and cannot stop myself.

"Nothing shall be lost. And when it is His, all of it, then he will rise in his million forms, across dimensions unimagined, to call out that one last message of His own. To let His Voice silence those insane flutes at the heart of the cosmos and break the Great Pretence."

"What will he say, mom?"

I squeeze closer to her, a mother telling her daughter the things a girl needs to know.

"He will stand before His Father, who tasks Him so woefully. The Father who demands that His own son should give service to order, and yet embody chaos. Our Faceless Lord will look into that false madness, and He will say..."

"With strange aeons, even You may die."

I kiss her, my heart erratic with pride.

"Yes. And with the death of the Father, there will be an end to all."

Kitty snuggles under my arm. This has always been her favourite story.

"And the Messenger will rest, at last," she whispers.

We will sleep, and there will be wondrous and terrible dreams. In the morning we will know His Will again, where we are to go next.

An end to all.

That is what happens when you do not show love for your child.

MOTHER'S NATURE

Stefanie Elrick

THE MAN IN THE LIMOUSINE WORE a white Egyptian cotton shirt.

It was the first clean thing I'd seen in a home saturated with slaughter and mud. No one came near my Uncle's farm, not if they could help it, hence the reason I'd sat amongst the shattered parts of man and beast for so long. Pain was a chord that hummed through the air there, the bellowing of the animals heard for miles around.

When he came, all was silent except for the soft purr of the engine as it approached. Generations of butchery had made my family more inbred than the cattle, now their limbs mingled indiscriminately with the livestock's. No one else had heard the screams, mine or theirs; of that I was certain.

He emerged from the backseat with a cool, fluid grace. Black sun-kissed skin and wide burnished eyes. The menthol freshness of the vehicle's interior hit me even from a distance, a synthetic tang that stung my nostrils and made me raise my gaze from the pattern I was tracing in the dust. Entrails squelched underneath designer shoes yet he seemed indifferent to the scene. I'd never seen anyone so beautiful. Spotless. Immaculate. He seemed to gleam. Lifting my taut little body up with long strong arms he placed me in the car. I curled like a clenched fist into its viscid leather and slept for the first time in days.

It's difficult to remember exactly what happened after leaving the farm. I have flashes of remembering, things that collide and combine in gusts of red and green, moments resistant to coherence. We travelled for days, or hours, and when I woke I was in a doll-filled room that smelt like antiseptic. Clamping my chin in his grasp he pushed green mush past my lips and the mess I made resisting irritated him. He scrubbed at the stains on my chest 'til my skin was red raw and I wailed like a baby. He never spoke a word. Trauma ricocheted through my system still and I fought like a cat held in a bucket. I'd resigned myself to death days earlier, so eating seemed like a meaningless task, another invasion of my will.

I do remember that he bathed me, holding me down in a high backed copper tub 'til I stopped struggling and calmed down. He cared for my body and quieted my chattering mind in all the practical ways a person can. Eventually his silent resilience put me at ease. I let him scrub away the years of neglect.

Finally sitting still, resigned not to kick or bite anymore, I noticed that I was bleeding, heavily, not from a wound but from my womb. I watched the haemoglobin snaking from my body, mingling delicately with the fresh clean water. How much finer it was than the lurid splatters that streaked the barn. None of us were squeamish, my cousins included, but when they'd seen my Uncle splayed open like an autopsy, wriggling in Its grip, they'd bolted like heifers.

I roughly pushed my fingers inside the soft mounds of my labia, deliberately not thinking of their blood but my own. He continued to wash the gore from my hair as aspic strands of jelly-fish tendrils hung from my fingers. All that blood, all that death, and nobody had survived but me.

When I slept that night I wove a patchwork of dreams. My mother came to me, covered in mildew and smiling through a mouthful of foam. She'd been sharpening her fingertips with a whetstone and I marveled at her cleverness, eagerly doing the same. We sat in silence, honing our bones to pointed pins, threading our hands with muscle stripped from her thighs. Overhead the sky was dying, brown oil slicks spreading across its surface. Time to start again. She promised me that nothing ever goes to waste and we stitched oceans to oceans as the clouds dropped like bombs. Floundering monsters opened heavy lids, then clambered on the land like babies learning to walk, dragging blankets of crimson waves behind them. Every gill-less thing that ever was suffocated under that mantle and we sat patiently, watching them sink, our fingers twitching in anticipation.

The next time I woke he took me to his workshop, a large room with small windows high above my head, covered with collages of animals and people. A sink and metal table stood in the corner with various knifes and tools nailed to the wall, above piles of uncut leather. Jars of murky embalmed things filled long shelves. A velvet curtain separated the studio from a shop, dimly lit and full of golden oval mirrors. A distinct white circle with arrows spiked from its perimeter was painted on the floor and adorned the window which overlooked a busy street, idyllically flanked by oak trees. Mannequins stood in rows with stuffed animal heads perched on willowy plastic necks. Clothing hung from their gaunt physiques at dramatic angles, garnished with pearlescent gemstones. The shop felt more like a museum than a boutique.

"Do you know what this is?" he asked, taking my hand and ignoring my flinches as he ran it over a coat.

I shook my head, as startled by his question as the sudden grip of his hand.

"It's crocodile skin, difficult to work with but highly rewarding. It's incredibly thick and tricky to stitch, has to be done by hand. Do you know what this is?" He moved my hand to a white trim. My ignorance embarrassed me.

"The pelt of an Arctic Wolf, so soft! The wolf itself does not keep it so well."

"What about this?" He smirked. This new material was rubbery, cold, like the sticky seats of the car. I winced as specks of blood welled on my fingertips.

He chuckled. "You will learn, little lamb. You like animals, don't you. We can make such beautiful things from their gifts, nothing should ever go to waste. Would you like to learn?"

I paused, overwhelmed by my sudden lesson.

"You're not stupid," he said, grabbing me again by the chin. "So, choose. You understand better than most the cycle of creation and destruction. The farm taught you things, didn't it? Nature is as brutal as she is beautiful." He paused thoughtfully, moving closer. "Sentimentality is a curse that animals do not suffer."

He released his grip and I nodded complicity to save face. Some kind of agreement had been struck.

At first I wondered if he'd force himself upon me; my Uncle and cousins had taught me well what man and beast desired most. But he never approached. He was only concerned with his work. As my trust grew, so did my lust. I was a woman now, with churning hormones and smouldering dreams, and we spent long nights alone in our candlelit studio. I grew possessive.

I wanted to impress him, show him what a seamstress and artist I had become through his instruction. If sculpting of flesh was the only way to do that then I vowed to surpass all his expectations. As well as skinning and cleaning the creatures that shifty men in blacked out vans delivered weekly, I began to preserve and bleach their bones, creating sculptures of delicate complexity. From a sparrow I made a tiny crescent moon, fixed to a pin he could wear on his lapel. From a horse's jawbone I carved a knife handle engraved with hieroglyphs from his most treasured book. When I had time to spare I practiced taxidermy, fashioning exotic chimera to present as gifts. With a paltry remark he might acknowledge my needlework or comment on the plausibility of the synthesis, yet I knew he was pleased as the shop filled with my experiments and even the customers remarked on my art. He would smile obliquely when asked if they were his and my pride swelled at the suggestion.

My training passed with the dizzy swiftness of a blossoming romance. I devoured books about evolution and discovered tomes exploring the rituals of zoolatry. We skinned and preserved all kinds of species and I watched him turn each into extravagant attire to be draped on human forms. He was an artist and a perfectionist, suturing skin into glorious amalgams. Clients came from all over the globe to buy his hybrid couture, and price was never a concern.

We had special customers too, ones who didn't seek our garments and mostly came at night. These fidgety bundles, barely preened and unable to articulate above grunts and nods, would wait until the shop was empty before being lead through a trap door to the 'fitting rooms' in the basement. Some emerged, eyes bright and skin glowing after a few hours, some after a number of days. Some I never saw leave.

I was never forbidden to enter the basement yet I was never invited either. In the early days I was eager not to displease, but of course it wasn't long before I found myself locking the shop and pulling back the heavy bulk of the trapdoor. He'd been down there for longer than usual, almost three days, with a drip of a woman not much older than myself. What kept him from our work for so long? I stared below, there was no sign of him or anyone else.

A phosphorous glow poured from the opening and I squinted in its caustic light. A long narrow corridor stretched to either side and the air down there was thick and hot. It smelt of sweat and shit, the same dank musk as the farm pens. Static shivered through the air, fondling the hairs on my scalp and my arms. A humid waft brushed my cheeks and on it travelled the groans of bovine beasts. I froze. My guts twisted, my senses pricked. Other muffled noises came from the corridor. Scratches, slaps, the sloshing of fluid. Cracking and panting and spontaneous laughter rose in soft crescendos before fading back into muffled whimpering. My temples throbbed, matching some unseen pendulum, and I moved down the steps, pulling the trapdoor closed behind me.

I walked for what could have been a mile on a floor lined with cracked stones and broken mosaics. The ground sloped up, as if I was climbing to the top of a hill, yet I never seemed to reach a peak or start descending. Tiny doors lined the corridor, the same pointed circle painted in a rusty brown above every one. They were so small that even I would have to crawl through them, with padlocks bigger than my hands.

The slapping and sucking intensified and a garish yellow light leaked from their tiny keyholes. Sometimes a frame would lurch as I passed, as if someone was throwing their weight against it from inside. I stopped, studying a pinkish fluid leaking under one threshold. The puddle smelt of brine and bleach and hissed quietly as it slid. I tried to peek through the keyhole, no bigger than my fingernail, but it was futile. A wet smack preceded a shuddering groan, then something like water spattering on a metal roof fell for minutes. Something gurgled, like water flowing down a drain. Who was in there, and was he inside too? Was he bathing that woman in the same way he had bathed me? Pride smouldered white hot.

"So you have found your way to the Emporium, little lamb?" he purred whilst exiting a door down the hall.

I stammered, and could summon no words, my jealousy hanging like a dead weight from my neck.

"You needed to know what was happening down here. A natural response. I was wondering how long it would take you." He smiled, putting a key in his pocket and wiping his hands on a lace handkerchief. "And you're ready now." Holding out his hand he lifted me from the floor. "This is the Flesh Emporium, where the most exciting parts of our work happens." For the first time since we'd met he took my arm like an equal and we strolled down the corridor as if walking through a park.

"Down here we cater to fantasies more juicy than vanity. We let explorers run wild, let them learn that boundaries are much more amenable than reason allows. Skin is malleable, a semi-permeable membrane, resilient. It stretches, absorbs, regrows, it can be refashioned. Flesh is a canvas at best. Would you like to see?" He paused at a door. I nodded, not wanting to show my unease. I bent down, ready to enter, then instantly backed away.

A skinless person, a woman or man, had been stripped to their muscle and was cradled in the grip of a hovering creature. Still alive, their eyes were wide and their mouth gasped madly for breath. Their skin hung just behind them, not torn or damaged, obviously carefully removed, and their body lay glistening like a new-born in its clutch. Arachnid arms of white jointed bone protruded from the creatures mass and it picked decisively at their flesh, humming scales of insectoid trills from a mouth jumbled with fangs. The thing had no eyes, and an exposed spine extending into a disjointed tail that thrashed from side to side. It dribbled in delight as it pulled the person apart, gelatinous salvia trickling from mandibles that burnt holes into the body, which twitched in response. Both victim and inflictor were absorbed in the work.

"When we use pain creatively we awaken sides of ourselves long since denied. Humans are gifted in destruction, yet they rarely use it to evolve. They slaughter indiscriminately, they rape what sustains them, they feast on all things and yet it does not enrich them. You understand, don't you, little lamb? You know how order is birthed from chaos. Look in here..."

He opened another door to my left and beckoned me forward. Inside, what looked like immense starfish were stuck to the walls, transparent spines on their backs filling with blood, like ticks. They pumped and ground their bodies obscenely and I noticed human shapes underneath. Hands and feet stuck out at all angles, fingertips flexing with each undulation.

"Are they eating them?" I whispered.

"Sometimes. If they want. It depends on what else there is to offer. These creatures have needs, they don't always desire the same thing. Some people come here to wear the flesh of others, to leave refined, reformed and redesigned. Some wish to be garments for the Old Ones; I treat them in the same way I treat our animal friends upstairs. Some simply beg to be obliterated, pushed to the edges of madness and then crushed into stardust. I open doors to those who delight in doing just that. Everything is consensual, everyone has a choice." He paused, watching me closely, as if waiting for a response.

"What do you choose, little lamb?"

I turned away as one of the twitching hands fell to the floor, shriveled and bloodless, leaving only a twisted stump of a wrist. My trembling voice disgusted me.

"I don't know."

"You have a gift, deep within you. A knowledge that far outweighs these dabblers. We are one, under the skin, the creators and the destroyers. You know this."

Electricity crackled in my sinuses and nausea swelled.

"I need to breathe," I mumbled.

"Do you? I'm not sure if you do. Let it happen," he soothed. "You are its Mistress, its lover. It's only energy, pure energy, waiting to be birthed into the world. We *are* One."

I bit my lip, trying to startle myself back to full awareness, but blackness closed in and my body went limp.

I awoke on the stone floor of a windowless room, the coolness of the rock soothed my throbbing head and I remained still for a long time. Sitting up, I saw shapes scrawled all over the walls, a tiny door closed in the corner. I was inside a chamber.

He sat in the corner on a low wooden stool, removing his jacket and waist coat, folding them neatly in a pile on the floor. Then he stood, removing his trousers and shoes until obsidian skin was all I could see. I'd dreamt of this for so long, yet now I felt like a child, timid and trembling, exposed and unsure.

He began to speak, his usual honeyed tones replaced by a cloying rasp. He sounded like he was drowning. I concentrated harder as guttural growls rose from his chest, felt blood rush to my groin. I trusted it instinctively, the rhythm of this visceral language, and as he flared with a blaze like uncorrupted starlight I could do nothing but draw closer to the flame.

The air smelled of wet soil and copper and his flesh began to simmer, slick and reflective. He gripped my mouth, nails embedding into my gums, lifting me up to his full height. As his incantation swelled the pores of the atmosphere yawned open, dripping jade secretions onto the floor, and our gazes locked as a spinning void of space rippled between us. I saw my fragile form, dangling jagged-boned and fretful, through his eyes. I was a weakened shell, a mess of shivering meat, brutalised and subliminally bruised by the shocks I had endured. This body was deformed, owned by its fear, bent and broken into intolerable angles and if it must be destined to perish then I welcomed destruction by his hand.

Thin black fissures formed on his face, splitting down his forehead and up the slope of his chin. Two more trailed across his cheeks until six met in the centre of his nose, then the whole façade split apart. Writhing triangles of rubbery flesh wriggled free as his head became a star covered in puckered suction cups, a blinding light pouring from a cat's eye slit in its centre.

He moved my hand to the centre of his chest, digging my fingernails into the tissue and ripping it away. He wanted to be stripped. I pulled the skin from his sternum, tearing his torso too, freeing the squirming innards eager to be released. My fingers slashed and grasped, growing slippery from his fluids until his new shape writhed around us, a mandala of twisting tendrils with tiny hooks at each end. They whipped and whirled against me, flaying skin from my bones. Now we were entangled, a mesh of limbs and meat. Everything shuddered ice cold.

Pain as pervasive as I'd ever known sharpened me into a lightning rod. I'd never felt so alive as I did in that second, weightless and naked in his monstrous grip. My body, a cross bow of agony, fired arrows into the dark heart of oblivion. Tentacles surged seeking secret crevices, tugging clumps of gristle systematically from my innards, jagged hunks of raw emotion that I'd let fester and cling to my organs. Guilt, shame, doubt, hesitance, jealousy, fear—he pulled them all from my body and tossed them like scraps to the void.

I saw us in that room, a conjoined mass of matter churning in a spherical cocoon. I saw all the rooms, saw the thrusting, slipping, dripping things feasting on each other and roving through the labyrinth of a dark communal mind. We all saw it, felt it all. Our minds hooked into a consciousness only versed in pain and obliteration.

I saw that night. Saw my Uncle's pelvis stabbing and jabbing and pushing its way into me. Semen and blood and fear in my mouth and the searing pain of a thousand similar conquests reverberating up my spine. Faces blurred and smeared indistinct until She appeared, enveloping all attention.

I saw her birth. A white hot spear shooting from my body, blazing from my third eye to my neck down my back and exploding from the void of my crotch. She was a hulk of clotted hurt, staggering forwards to the source of her pain, an eyeless wound of a face split open revealing row upon row of bloody, shattered teeth. With harpy claws she tore at her hair, capillary networks fanning like wings from her back. She hurled my Uncle's body against the floor, impaling him with a tongue suddenly stretched into a spike. Then she screamed, a vile gargling shriek that spat hunks of meat onto his petrified face. My voice, her voice, giving form to every wretched thing that ever suffered without consent. His flesh flew away from the impact of her sorrow and the farm became a maelstrom of ripping, twisting, unforgiving energy. Everything flew apart: the barn, the cows, the dogs, the pigs, my Uncle, my cousins. Me. Everything exploded with the sincerity of her pain.

I felt his body judder from the weight of her presence. Now every ounce of will he had was forced into me. I shattered like a nebula, spewing razor shards of light across the Universe. Every string of my psyche and all the dark communes sang that we were one.

We were One.

We

Are

One

It took a long time to rebuild myself after he left me in that room. Not as long as the first time, I'm sure, but then it's hard to recall. At first my awareness hung in a sentient mist, fused gently to every particle of air around it and nothing more. There was a strange satisfaction to that state, light and clean, holding nothing but the weight of air and moisture.

I suppose it was inevitable that my ego would prevail, that the idea of my own importance would infiltrate space and I'd start to flourish. The simplicity couldn't last; evolution is an obstinate beast. At the farm I'd believed it was over, that I'd finally found a sanctuary in the stillness, away from the nightmare life I'd known. But something had murmured me back together then, and this time I murmured to myself, willing that kernel of being to dream of a deeper purpose, something slipping past my consciousness as fluid and persuasive as the tide.

I nurtured my seed, focused on the multiplying of cells, and knitted myself slowly whole with the needle of my will. Since my initiation I remembered much more than my mortal self ever could and I'd lots of time to recall in that suspended loop. The more I remembered the denser I became until disparate particles starting bumping together, creating the friction and warmth needed to condense. I became a puddle, a plasma pool of poetic potential, and from this embryonic water, mixed with our blood, I pulled myself up, forcing bones to calcify and organs to grow. My heart began to pump, and I developed, curled in a bud of becoming, held in the palm of the Old Ones.

I remembered what They remembered, I dreamt their bloody dreams. I saw the apocalyptic ends of a thousand worlds and felt them, rebuilding and rejuvenating in their fathomless nests. How many times had they risen from their slumber? Resurrected from eons of sleep to crown the world's madness. The desperate soul of Nature summoned them time and time again and they rose to vanquish her foes, lest she break under their demands. They had ripped the world asunder, drowned it in floods, feasted on its children, scorched it with flaming rocks. Afterwards, it was forced to grow again, and they retreated, to observe from the tattered edges of reality. Gaia's shadow, her lovers, harbingers of the New Dawn.

Now I know with absolute certainty that when the time comes I will be there, open hearted and wide as the sky, as their Priestess and their Guide and an Architect of the Flesh. I will pluck up the fragments discarded in their wake, lick the wounds of the broken, and teach them the wonder of destruction. New humanity will be my masterpiece, my most inspired work of art.

Without the skin, we are One.

.

Mr. JOHNSON and the OLD ONES

Jamie Mason

— pour Kiernan, en hommage

Ω

STANDING HERE, O LORD, WITH my guitar in my hand at this crossroads, I feel a cold wind at wrist and knee where my trousers done frayed, and the black soil clutching one foot through the sole of one worn shoe. Something tells me, O Lord, that He is coming. Beneath the cold moon, as sure as the smell of burned leaves and fresh pumpkins and warm entrails rises on the harvest wind, He interrupts His timeless sleep beneath the waves and journeys from His dreaming city to this same place same time each year, breaking bleak and terrible upon this alien shore.

O Lord, I done sold my soul long ago. To you, in fact, in exchange for my talent on this guitar. The stroke of a pen refined me to a silver wire wound tight and set to vibrate like a new *E* string whenever your fingers move upon it so I play, O Lord. This machine summons storms.

I am strong enough now. I move between worlds, speaker for the Dust of Vermin unto the Old Ones. Strong, but also because they love me.

They dream, and love music to accompany their dreaming.

Are we so different?

7

From banks of blackened stone, I watch fog coalesce across the sound. By tradition I stand at a crossroads, as when I first met you, O Lord. But *this* crossroads belongs to Him by tradition, being beside the ocean.

I bring the guitar across my body. I can tell it's tuned by feel, by smell, by the way the tightened, straining wood settles against my chest. I am more connected to this instrument, to my music, than I am to the reality of this present moment, O Lord, and all those yearnings turn Your way through bleak and breaking winter light. I breathe and remember and hurt and my fingers fall to the strings and music rises like the agony of silver angels crucified within the caverns of my Gibson:

> *yeah can't you hear that wind howl?*
> *you can hear it now*
> > *oh when a woman gets in trouble...*

The surface of the water done begins to quake. A hyperborean glow churns the currents from below, just as the skies above roil in response to my playing. Something so ancient and huge and bioluminescent cannot rise to this depth unless atmospheric conditions are correct and all the doorways—between R'lyeh and this dimension's ocean, between sea and sky, between this world and the planet these ancient creatures call home—have been opened.

> *...everybody throws her down*

I feel the sweet ache as my fingers move and seek their accustomed chord-shapes and the notes take their groove and the steel stings perfect little notes into the sky. There are no words. And the Old Man does not rise to the surface. His coming within a thousand miles is enough to snap my mind against the knife-edge of madness. And so the melody widens and distorts and my voice blazes and cracks along volcanic fissures, as it so often does these days, allowing Its new song to emerge:

you better cthulhu r'lyeh wgah'ngal fhtagn
in my kitchen...

Speaker between worlds.

...because it's going to be raining outside

My voice, the Dust of Vermin crying unto the Old Gods of the Dreamless City, clamoring about the foot of the steps to their ancient temple. I sing and the entirety of humanity's longing falls upon the ears of those for whom we are but a ghostly dream.

E♭

Clap-board shack, O Lord, built shotgun-style right there at the crossroads—a different one from where I'd sung by the sea, O Lord, but all crossroads are alike, just as every jook house is the same. We all know these places, Lord, built by music and liquor and luck where dice rolls and blood flows and the stench of jealousy and lust rises like sweet incense to You. It's where I make my stand each night, O Lord.

The little gate squeaks as I push through and cross the trash-strewn yard to the steps. A black hound by the door raises his head and watches my approach. Recognizing me as one of Your own, O Lord, he lets me pass into the parlor.

The curtains are drawn but I see dust hanging in a shaft of light. Down the hall is the jook room with the stage and dance corral but up this end of the corridor are a few rooms the girls work. The obeah woman sits guarding the red door.

"He here." She nods toward the opposite door, a pitch pine painted a stark yellow in the wall beside the fireplace. "He done showed a mojo hand so I let him in. Like the Old Man said to do."

I nod slow, tuning my guitar.

"It won't be long now." The obeah woman's hand drops to a scattering of coins, some burned tobacco and chicken bones on her lap. "The stars say a daughter. We'll know soon enough. Did the Old Man send you?"

I don't answer.

"You go *on*, be that way, Mister Robert," the obeah woman chuckles. "But a woman like me done delivered you and a woman like me will comfort your dying bed, praise the Old Man of the Mountains of Madness. Your puttin' on airs don't make no nevermind to me!"

My guitar is tuned. I am ready for battle.

"What's he called, this visitor man?"

"He done left a calling card all proper and gentleman-like." Producing it from the pocket of her apron, she hands it to me.

H. P. LOVECRAFT

"What's he claiming for himself, this Lovecraft?"

"He say he come from the local school. Said he the Principal." The obeah woman rearranges her skirts primly. "Come to take care of a truancy problem."

The yellow door breathes as I approach. I know a Shine when I see one so I play. Just a few notes: enough to take the edge off the hex before I touch the knob. It turns easily, like it's been oiled, but it hasn't. Hasn't nothing been oiled in this house in years 'cept the kerosene lamps I can smell stepping my way through the door.

A small, cluttered sitting room: a spinning wheel in one corner, a sofa jammed in the other. There's a crowd of burlap bags crowding one wall, Lord, and I see cotton in there, and laundry and bales of knick-knacks and peoples' clothing and personal effects and books and magazines like the ones on the table over which the man leans, reading, his back turned, shoulders of his dark suit narrowing like a black triangle to a slender waist. He pivots toward me, eyes narrowing. Although he is tall, I note the little round glasses, the weak mouth. There's something sickly, frail about the man.

"So. They sent a nigger!"

I been called worse. Much. I touch an open string, just to see how he reacts when the note sounds. Do it in such a way that it looks like an accident in case one of his Seniors take offense, which they don't (although the light outside the window darkens briefly).

"I'm the *Principal*. There's a girl who's supposed to be in *school* right now and she's *not*, so I've come to collect her."

"You're a little early." I finger-pick a lazy *D*. "She ain't been born yet."

"Well, you niggers *are* a lazy bunch. Always behind schedule."

"Mm-hm."

I begin a slow blues with a walking bass-line. Just a single note: *thut—thut—thut...* Just like that. It appears to get under his skin the teensiest bit.

"You imagine that hoodoo music is powerful enough to spook me?"

"Depends. You powerful? You important?"

"I have published stories in magazines."

"You mean like the *New Yorker*?"

"*Not* like the *New Yorker*!" He makes a fist. "Not *yet*, anyway!"

"Well, then why haven't I heard of you?"

"Can you read?"

"Sure. I reads de *New Yorker* all the time, boss."

"Well, they're not buying my stories like they used to! I think it's because too many women and darkies are writing these days. Seems people would rather pay a nickel for a pulp rag full of messages about race and gender instead of the good old-fashioned adventure stories I was raised on that made our culture great!"

"Mm-hm."

I keep the bassline going and start up with a little chicken-picking.

"We're a culture of heroes! Not... beasts. *Must you continue playing that nigger music?*"

Instead of answering I flash a dazzling, wide-toothed nigger smile and sing:

> *she's a kind-hearted woman*
> *studies evil all the time...*

"Yes, go ahead. Sing your gibberish. Spout your doggerel, ape-creature."

she studies evil all the time
you wells to kill me as to have it on
your mind...

"If you sung of heroes instead of elevating the base lusts of man, perhaps you'd be somewhere nobler than grubbing in the dirt and feeding your children to the Mi-Go!"

I cut off mid-phrase.

There is a certain kind of Black man's anger that can silence a bigot. I see that self-same fear crawl Lovecraft's face. Alone in a room in a strange whorehouse with a black man in the middle of nowhere, anything could happen to his skinny white ass and he knows it.

"The loss of our children is a sacrifice we willingly make for the entire *world*."

"Not this time. I have other plans for this Pickaninny."

"Other plans?"

"She'll be food. Sacrificed to the *right* monstrosity, not whatever ally of convenience one of your obeah mistakenly conjured into existence!"

I reflect on the woman guarding the door in the parlor outside. She's like to have never made a juju mistake in her entire life. Can't read nor write but precise as a surgeon where it comes to matters of the spirits.

And the Tribute.

"That child was born for one purpose, Mr. Lovecraft. You know this because you set the terms of the cosmic battle. Here on Earth, the slumbering Old Gods. There on Pluto, the Mi-Go, perched in their high towers, poised to invade."

The bigot waves a hand. "*What of it?*"

"So then you must know the terms of the truce. We are to provide a newborn once every sixty-six days, when the moon is in Yuggoth!"

"Fantasy!" Lovecraft emits a nervous titter. "In those days I was overly concerned with matters of the imagination and less preoccupied than I should have been with the business side of publishing. That child—" he points "—is worth a small fortune on the black market to a certain barren, up-scale couple I know. That money will allow me an entrée to circulate amongst those who can open my way to the elite."

"If the Mi-Go do not receive their Tribute they lay waste to the Earth!"

"A small oversight we can rectify later..."

"Excuse me? The destruction of the Earth? A *small* oversight?"

"We'll make it up to them in six years' time when we bring *two* infants. And in the meantime I can use *this* one to become rich and famous. What is the life of a nigger babe compared to wealth and riches?"

"What good are wealth and riches when the planet is a cinder?"

"I wouldn't expect you to understand, being a nigger. My plans require risk and ambition. Sloth and stupidity are your two most well-known failures as a race."

"Well that's as may be, massa Lovecraft, but it don't take no big heap of intelligence to see that a dead planet is a high price to pay for one man's personal ambition."

My right hand falls to the pistol in my coat pocket.

No bluesman walks around the Mississippi Delta without carrying no pistol.

I pull mine cool and slow and level it on the narrow, cachectic chest behind which Howard Philips Lovecraft's cowardly heart beats and cock the hammer.

"Now you listen here, you stupid white man. You and me we're pawns in a game being played by the gods. Either choice is bad because a child dies but we have it in our power to make sure she dies for the right reason. Doesn't that mean anything to you?"

"Whatever it means is higher than whatever it means to a nig—"

"Okay."

I raise up my pistol and my hands and step out through the yellow door to the parlor where the obeah woman sits contemplating the scatter of coins, ash and bones in her lap.

"*Wait!*"

Lovecraft stumbles out behind me with a kind of jerky, primitive urgency. He is all arms and elbows, gangly hips and knees.

"Grant me one wish!" His voice is peremptory. He feels himself entitled to it, whatever he is about to ask for, so he asks in a demanding way.

"What is it?"

"Grant me one sight of Her." Lovecraft raises his chin importantly. "The Great Sow. She who feeds the Mi-Go! The Bearer of the Damned."

The obeah woman frowns. "You sure you want to see that?" she asks.

"I AM!"

Weren't those the sacred words, O Lord, by which Jehova God proclaimed himself to Moses?

"You are?" The obeah woman blinks. "You are that you are?"

Why would any man ask to see Her? Why risk staggering out to the edge of sanity, O Lord, where the high cliffs of Reason reel out over the gulf of stars? Why risk a glimpse into the Abyss? But perhaps Lovecraft doesn't see it that way. Perhaps he thinks behind the door the obeah woman guards is just another black whore got banged up and getting set to deliver a black bastard. Maybe he figures he'll catch a hint of flesh, of something memorable he can call up in his mind's eye on a lonely winter night as he reaches for himself beneath the covers...

What's behind that door is memorable, alright.

The obeah woman reaches out and twists the handle. The door falls open.

And it does fall. It doesn't yawn or widen or belly or swing. It *falls*. Because the wall cantilevers and tilts, flattening to become the floor and then stretching and distorting into a yawning scarlet pit in the midst of which something vast and horrible pulses and twists like a great artery pushing blood, or an intestine pushing waste. The totality of the appalling vision of the She-goat giving birth, only this is no goat, nor no she, nor so recognizable thing of Earth. This was

is

a

vertigo

birth of something so...

To gaze upon the horrible engine of nature, that vast and shivering fecund being who is the Great Sow, to witness her pulsing cloaca and shuddering arteries is to see the greater process of universal birth brought eternal—to peer into the red wound of Time, itself—a sight to beggar even the firmest reason.

And so Lovecraft, transfixed, glares downward into the unfolding scarlet Coriolis of the Great Sow's birthing, witnessing the impossible succession of offspring, mind reeling as Her greatness and profundity strike him with all the subtlety of an avalanche and all the strength of an Autumn leaf wafting on the afternoon wind of downtown Providence...

Lovecraft's screams rip and tear and echo across the totality of the jook house parlor to touch the edges of the universe beyond.

Raving and gibbering, he is apprehended by the Shadow Police and taken to the Tribunal of the Trapezoid within the Forbidden City of R'lyeh. But like all other humans, any hope of his sentencing dies immediately upon arrival for no sooner does Lovecraft gaze upon the incomprehensible architecture of the Dreaming City than his mind shatters decisively and he descends for the last time into the labyrinth of eternal madness.

A^{7th}

It is a dark night, Lord. Dark as all ever was.

And so I wait, Lord. Even hiding in the ditch when the lights of some trucks draw close, O Lord, because their eyes smell like demons' and I ain't in no kind to get stuck of these, O Lord.

I have witnessed the Great Sow regurgitate the black Earth of corruption into renewed light.

I have stared down through the Earth for a glimpse of Her Kingdom.

I have seen into the heart of the Old Ones, O Lord. A profound, world-shaking uncertainty grips me, about everything I know or have come to believe is strong and unassailable. Even your strength, Lord, O my Lord.

And so the night goes on until day breaks. Light fills the hole at the top of the stone dome and washes downward in a shaft filled with chicken feathers and spider webs...

i went down to the crossroads, o lord,
tried to flag a ride ...

AT the LEFT HAND of NOTHING

Jayaprakash Satyamurthy

WE WORK OUR WAY TO THE COLD, hard nothing at the heart of it all. We work our way through stations of the crooked:

first comes the foreswearing of all former oaths and fealty

second comes the destruction, with élan and malice, of a stranger

third comes the act of mass violence, known to the worldly as terrorism

fourth comes the utter degradation of a loved one

fifth comes the betrayal of the self, and this is a lifelong mission

(but there is one even more exalted, more on that later)

There are those among us for whom these are steps towards a final revelation, terrible but True, and therefore worth having. These acolytes may prove to be useful fools, but they never last very long or rise very high. They still hold to some semblance of a value system and of a quest for anything other than blasphemous annihilation. They are still of the world, of the cosmos, and not fully awake. True anamnesis has eluded them.

Those of us who have risen in truth from our slumber, who have seen consciousness for the tarnished coin that it is, and have seen the world and the things that slumber or stumble or pipe and ululate above and beyond it for what they are, we are an inner elite with a clear and supreme goal.

My own awakening was equal parts pain and ecstasy, which is par for the course. I can describe it, but the description may lack the precision and clarity available to accounts of more quotidian experiences. Certainly, tentacles are an apt metaphor for what goes on, although there is no corporeal component to their probing, entering, fecundating and scarificating appendages. It is like being caressed and molested and violated and vindicated, all at once and forever. As my agony-orgasm blossomed, I knew that all my ideas were wrong, that all my premonitions and intuitions had misled me. I knew that, even if logic and reason somehow adhered somewhere in the cosmos, I did not have the tools with which to fathom them. I gave myself up to the alienated heart of it all, to the widdershins beat that syncopates in a space right at the centre and far, far outside.

Most of my fellow initiates emerge from this salutary ordeal awakened to some degree, but still deluded because their faculties are, in the crunch, too tenacious. If the experience drives you a little insane, it is only because you have not fully embraced it, because you still have structures and complexes in your psyche which are capable of such derangement. These poor lunatics become our useful fools: these are the ones who chant, and incantate, and hold rituals in swamps or dockside basements.

There is an entire literature out there dealing with the antics of these fools. It is imagined that these plots and cults are the sum of our ambition; that we exist merely to subvert normality and exalt some strange pantheon, that we want to bring a triumphal return of squamous divinity to old Earth.

This, in summary, is what we may call the Right Hand Path of Nothingness. It is diverting, it has some utility in destabilizing things, always a fine endeavour, but it is as fundamentally mistaken as the notion that there must be meaning at the heart of anything.

Some of us are able to take it further; the tentacles, if you will, have slithered deeper within and we ourselves are now tentacled. And we probe and fold space with our new conceptual appendages and we see just how much more perfect the insanity of it all may become.

We sit in rooms lit with burning grimoires, stacks of paper currency and art afire, we sit in rooms rank with blood and ordure, ripe with odours of decay and fragrances of musk and honey and heliotrope, we confer in chambers lined with bones and flayed skin, we conspire in hollows within immense beings captured in spaces between spaces and times between times, we listen to the mellifluous caterwauling of our pinioned mothers and fathers and husbands and sisters and strangers and we calmly, frenetically, plan the sixth station of the crooked.

The fall of Cthulhu. Nyarlathotep's final dance. Shub-Niggurath's unbirthing. Yes, even Yog-Sothoth's awakening into final oblivion. Call it what you will. We have destroyed all our humanity, reveled in death and blood and despair, stalked down the Left Hand Path toward bleak revelation without flinching and all these things were only appetizers to the real feast. We have seen, in the words of an earthly sage, that the meaning of life is that it ends. *It ends.* Life ends, and even that which is not dead may someday die.

The name of our calling is deicide. When the stench of burning gods' flesh fills the cosmos with charnel reek, when divine ordure clogs the streets and plains of every world, when the carcasses of the pantheon litter all of space and time, we will have taken our madness to its logical conclusion. The time is coming; we are sure of this. So we lie low, in our chambers of horror and madness, we linger lovingly over feasts of scream and scorn and watch the puppets twitch on their strings, and stand in wait for the gods.

Every one of us a snare and a gallows, waiting at the left hand of nothing for the day of their return.

THAT MOST FOREIGN of VEILS

LUKE R. J. MAYNARD

THE BABY SCREAMED IN ITS mother's arms the whole way there, as if it alone could understand Sabiha's darkness of purpose. The brutish security guards in Paris had thought they understood, but her purpose lay too deep for their molesting hands to find. The white man seated to her right—a loud chewer who had fixed his disgusting curiosity on her eyes for most of the second flight—he thought he knew. To her left, faithful Ghada thought she knew, too. But even the bond of sisterhood did not open to her the burden of the howling wind. Ghada had too much of her new home in her, now—besides which, her old home in Sana'a was not so remarkable either, for those who did not look deep. She had told Ghada once—in the language of science, cellular language she thought a chemist would understand—that the Earth was rather like Great-Grandfather, a thing of exceeding and unfathomable age below, but wrapped in a wrinkled skin at most two or three weeks old.

"You think the skin is exceedingly old," she had said, "only it isn't —not really."

Paris had only been the midpoint of their journey. There, in a steel room crowded with cameras, Sabiha removed her veil for a big woman with a bullish scowl who looked on her face, and touched her body roughly, and searched through her handbag with the crassness of a goat grazing in trash. She, too, was a skin cell upon the Earth, a living part of a tremendous fabric of light patches and dark, smoothness and scars— yet something to be sloughed off, when the time came. If even Great-Grandfather could be sloughed off in his final days, so could anyone. And his remaining days in the world had turned now to mere hours, unless there was something more in the stars; that, in vulgar shorthand, was the reason for her trip.

Every step of the way, just as it was in Yemen, those with temporal power thought they understood, and were always mistaken. It was one thing, perhaps the only thing, they had in common with this strange cold land, far from ordinary people, at the end of the world. The blindness of the strong and the wisdom of the weak were the same the whole world over, and that grim fact put her at ease somehow. It made the whole of the trip, from the stale air of plane after plane to the alien frost of Toronto, feel a little less uncanny.

But the screaming baby knew. The babies always knew.

"I wish Great-Grandfather would learn to use the Internet," said Ghada, shattering the surrounding static of half-understood English with her familiar words. "It's not fair, I know. But you could see him, and speak to him, and say your farewells from a café in Aden. Why you both refuse to learn these things is beyond me. If Great-Grandfather wants to die without a computer or television, it's fine. I cannot criticize a man who never even warmed to the printed codex. But you are a young woman, Sabiha, and the world is bigger than you know."

At the next gate, another uniformed guard spat some English in a voice demanding obedience.

"Step this way," said Ghada. "You've been selected for another random screening." Her eyes narrowed. She didn't seem to think it was random at all.

"It's their right," said Sabiha, dutifully stepping behind a line of yellow tape. "They are only being careful."

Ghada blinked sharply. "No, you've traveled only two days. You would tire of it very quickly, this hellish carefulness. It gets into your clothes and your hair, in time, the way they treat you. It's why I don't make the trip home anymore, except to fetch you this one time. It's why you'll be going back alone."

"Ghada, you can't be serious!"

"It will be fine. *Ummuna* and Nadheer will get you at the airport."

Sabiha sighed her disapproval. "It's terrible."

"All travel in the West is like this," said Ghada. "I love my sister. Of course I am glad to see you. But you have only begun to learn why you should not have come."

"I'm not afraid," said Sabiha. *Not of that*, she added to herself.

It was two hours before they cleared customs, for reasons neither sister could understand. The dim afternoon had already darkened to night, and luminous fat flakes of snow seemed to race each other to the earth in the orange glow of the lights over the parking lot.

"It's so cold," said Sabiha. "What time is it?"

"It's early, yet," said her sister. "We've got a long way to go."

Sabiha eyed her sister with surprise. "You're driving?"

Ghada gestured to the snow. "Well, we're not walking," she said in English.

The pickup truck was new and shiny, but it turned over sluggishly in the cold. Sabiha cringed as her sister held the key over and forced the engine to something like life.

"Don't break it," said Sabiha. "Nadheer would say, you mustn't break it."

Ghada smiled and let go of the grinding key as the engine smoothed out. "He would also say, you mustn't talk about things you don't know. Canada is my country now, Sabiha. Things are different here. And put on your seat belt."

"Not so different," said Sabiha. "Men are the same most everywhere. Here, women just go about more like men. Do you suppose that makes them easier to understand, or harder?"

"You do not understand my world," snapped Ghada.

"Nor you mine."

They drove in sulking silence for a long time. Resentment turned to silent boredom as the sisters sat alone with their thoughts. Ghada watched the white highway streak by and half-dreamt of a bespectacled man with green eyes that sparkled like gems. He worked in her laboratory, and she wondered if Sabiha might put in a good word with the family, if only she tolerated her sister's absurd journey. She resented them, a little, and wondered if their approval would be so important now. She liked the food here, and had learned all there was to know about winter, and wondered whether she would ever leave.

Far away, on the other side of the truck cab, Sabiha pondered just how little Ghada really knew about winter. She had read many books in the sciences, perhaps, but Sabiha knew that books could no more capture the sound of the wind than a pinned insect the mystic truth of its flight. It would never be quite right, in the end—and thinking about it, once it was written, could drive you mad.

"How far is it to Great-Grandfather's house?" asked Sabiha, when her thoughts had turned to fluttering nightmares, and all the silence she could stand had passed.

"Far as far, and half again," said Ghada. "I have seen it only once, to put him there in the first place. If you understood where we must go, you would never have asked it of me."

"You do not want to take me."

"Of course not," snapped Ghada. "But you are my only sister, and the old fool's only friend. He can hide from all the world, but he cannot hide from the Hour. And no one should die alone."

"Even death may die," breathed Sabiha, caressing the pendant beneath her abaya.

"What was that?" asked Ghada.

"I asked, how far is the drive?" Sabiha lied. "It seems like we have driven for hours."

"We have," said Ghada. "We will be in Cochrane by morning. But the drive is only the beginning."

They passed an endless procession of Western towns, all dominated by squat brick houses and low blocky industrial buildings with dull metal siding. The Christian cathedrals that seemed so vain and grandiose in the city gave way to smaller, humbler facsimiles—queer triangular buildings of snow-covered brick and wood. The low rolling fields turned to immense walls of hard brown rock, through which the long white ribbon of road had slashed like a searing knife. True to Ghada's word, they pulled into Cochrane just after sunrise. In this last morning light, she saw before Ghada replaced her veil that she had aged some, though she was still exquisitely beautiful.

In town, Ghada's English became so rapid-fire with the white men that Sabiha was lost in its bellowing sharpness. They were in a trainyard, loading the truck onto an impossibly long train, paying in thin wads of skinny plastic bills. Above them the wind howled strangely, and Sabiha knew that they had come to a doorway. Great-Grandfather had not lied when he said he was going beyond that most foreign of veils to hear the last verse of the song of the dead. Only now, in these frigid gatelands, did she understand him.

There was more money to come, lots of it. Sabiha had some idea of what it would have bought in Yemen. At a giant yellow discount store by another triangular church, Ghada bought her a winter coat without haggling over price, and maybe without even looking at it. She clucked her tongue dismissively when Sabiha tried to protest.

"I already have a coat," said Sabiha.

"You may think that's a coat," said her sister. "You'll learn soon enough that it isn't."

"I'm only shivering because I'm up all night."

"You'll sleep on the train, and then you'll see that's not so."

In a small restaurant, Ghada with her meticulous English ordered them a breakfast of eggy bread that was something like a plain mutabbaq in a sweet syrup, and they returned to meet a passenger train that looked smaller and far more frightened of the North than its freight-hauling cousin. On plastic seats, jostling over uneven ties, Sabiha lay her head against the rattling window and drifted into sleep as the train trundled away from a country that only hours before had seemed alien to her.

The snow in her dreams may as well have been the white sands of the desert. According to the old hadiths, hellfire could burn both cold and hot; as a child, Sabiha had assumed that if you went round one way far enough, you could reach the other. Great-Grandfather had always flourished in the hellish desert; she recalled now once how she had gone to see him near Damascus as a young girl, she had returned home with her brown hands so badly sunburnt that they shed their skin again and again, like the skin of a desert reptile. He had been a young man of eighty-some years then, and she just a girl. In her dream she was thirteen, sitting on a threadbare carpet in his home, sharing sweets with him from an enormous platter laid out on a woven mat. Great-Grandfather had always had the best sweets; it was, when she was very young, what had made him interesting. But at thirteen, her thoughts had changed.

"Always you eat so many sweets," she said. "How are you so thin when all you eat is honey and cake?"

"I have told you," said Great-Grandfather. "There is a hollowness in me as big as the sky."

"I said the same thing to my mother," she said. "She does not believe it." He only smiled in answer.

She wondered somehow, in the dream, whether these were memories—whether it was a conversation they had had that summer, or whether she only dreamt it now, or whether it had always been there, forgotten, in someplace beyond the noise of the old city. In the dream she took the last cake and chewed it thoughtfully.

"When will you teach me the all the secrets of the wind?"

"All of them?" said Great-Grandfather. "When you turn into a hundred curious children, and when I become a hundred old and dying men."

"Nadheer says you're old and dying now."

"Nadheer speaks the truth," said Great-Grandfather. "Though he does not know it. You are old and dying, too, Sabiha."

"Then when can I know it all?"

"Even I don't know it all," said Nadheer. "It's madness to think of it. I mean it, madness. One day, I will tell you the story of the man who tried to write it all down."

"When, Great-Grandfather? When?"

"When you too hear the wind that howls from beyond the veil, child. When you know a little of why he failed."

"So...after the new year?"

"Yes," he said. "A long time after that."

When the journey's end jostled her awake, the smells of his old house were still fresh in her mind. She wondered how long it had been from that moment to this, and could have counted to her present age, but simple arithmetic would not answer her question. Great-Grandfather had seemed ninety then, she thought, but she wasn't sure. Like an unmarried woman in the market, his true age was an impossible mystery. He might only be ninety now. But if he were only ninety, she thought, he had been ninety for a very long time.

Still with one foot in dream, she clutched her new sleeves tightly and came out of the train with Ghada. A light snow was falling, fat flakes the size of beetles shining peach-pink under the tall station streetlights. Beyond the thin veil of streetlit snow, the day was as black as a crypt.

"What time is it?" Sabiha asked, shivering.

"North," answered her sister.

The cold of snowy Toronto was the distant memory of a summer's day by comparison, so far behind them that she wondered if she had made up the whole thing. Perhaps Toronto had been this cold, after all. Perhaps the desert roads of Yemen were this cold, too. Perhaps it was this cold, all over the world, and always had been, and would be till the very end.

They met the truck at the freightyard across the lot, and sat shivering and burning fuel for a time. Sabiha gripped her pendant tightly. It was nearly hot against her skin, now, and kept the fingers from going numb. She might have fallen asleep again, if Ghada had not wrenched the truck into low gear to follow the truck she had been waiting for—a supply truck with bright tail lights, turning up toward the ice road.

"I understand you, now," said Sabiha. "This *is* a long way."

Ghada smiled. "We haven't driven across the ocean to nowhere, yet. Don't forget your seat belt."

The ice road came only in winter, and only then when the sheet ice over the bay was thick enough to support a supply truck. This was no easy task, for this was no simple lake road, but an uncanny blue-white highway pushing a tireless path across the sea itself. The water here was deep and salty; only a few weeks a year would the road appear. It was a dangerous way, and grew more dangerous every year as some unseen hand of cruelty transformed the world. They drove painfully slow, nothing but flat ice and blackness around them, save the distant tail lights of an experienced rig in the distance—but he soon outpaced them, and then there was nothing. Ghada told her sister, as the drivers had told her, to proceed with a hand on the door at all times, and to be ready to leap onto the ice and crawl away from the truck if she felt the front-end lurch down violently. They might survive on the ice for a half hour or so; the chances of a passerby in that time might be slim, but it was a better end than the deep.

That much Sabiha did not need to be told twice. There was a special end to those who went below, especially in these places beyond the world. She understood, only now, that her sister had not been so unwise, so utterly unschooled in the howling of the wind. She could hear it in the infinite black above them, now that it was too cold even for snow, screaming against the cab of the truck.

"Your courage is great in coming here," said Sabiha.

"I'm past courage and into madness," said Ghada, knuckles tight on the wheel, one hand on the door. "It runs in the family. I'm crazy as Great-Grandfather. Crazier, even. I can't imagine why he came up here to die. But there's a certain sense, when you go somewhere to die, choosing a place that will kill you. I don't yearn for such things, Sabiha. I yearn for my book to be published, and for handsome Jason in my laboratory to notice me, and for Nadheer to approve of my marrying a Westerner someday. All things that will not happen if we go down through the ice. Everything Great-Grandfather wants in death, he is going to get. Everything Ghada wants in life, Ghada's going to lose."

There was a warmth in Ghada's complaining, as if they were young together again, as if two sisters lamenting the unkindness of life to each other were the most natural and human thing in the world. They passed the timeless journey as the kindred sisters they had once been, and their laughter warmed the cab at last. It was dark beyond dark, now, and the headlights and instruments and the two women's smiles gave off the only light in all existence, like a single dwarf star trembling in the merciless void of night.

On the far side of eternity lay a town. A few flickering lights there carried a long way into the cloudless, snowless night. Beneath their welcoming glow, the ice road turned again to gravel and wound through rows of metal homes like tiny airplane hangars. The Northern store where they parked the truck looked like the same design, built of the same materials—only scaled up like a mothership.

"Remember we are only guests on this land," said Ghada. She raised her veil and tied her scarf over it. It took several hard pushes to unstick the frozen doors.

It was clear Ghada expected her to be uncomfortable here, but after the long night on the ice road, the supermarket was like coming home. The fluorescent lights offered the illusion, at least, of warmth, and the women who shopped among the onions and crates of oranges were likewise attired—leggings under long dresses, immense puffy coats, heads wrapped under hats, faces scarved, eyes beautiful and glistening like dark gems. It was the first place in the West she felt as if she could have talked to anybody, even in English.

Ghada bought them some fruit that had once been fresh. Sabiha could tell from her sister's body language that it was very expensive. But it gave her an excuse to talk to the cashier, a pretty raven-haired girl who looked surprised to see them, but not wary.

"I'm looking for Michael Billy," said Ghada, handing over her purchases. "Do you know him?"

The girl nodded. "You're here to see the Arab," she said, smiling brightly with recognition. "Both of you?" It was a kinder reaction, here at the top of the world, where maybe no Arabs had ever been but Great-Grandfather, than Sabiha had seen anywhere in the city that supposedly housed fifty thousand of them.

"Yes," said Ghada.

"I'll find Mike for you," she said. The clerk at the next register rang them through as the girl bounced away, and Ghada exchanged pleasantries while Sabiha studied the store, transfixed by the bright colours after what felt like a century of night.

The girl's cheeks were rosy from the cold when she returned, bringing a round-faced man with shaggy hair and a catfish smile, dressed up like a pillbug in a puffy blue coat with, of all things, a baseball cap.

"Hey stranger," he said in English. "It's been a long time."

"Hello," said Ghada. Sabiha could tell she was disarmed by the man's friendliness; she was, too, a little.

"And this is your first time," he said. "I'm Mike. I've been looking after the old man." Sabiha extended a gloved hand timidly, as she had been taught, and he shook it hard and enthusiastically. It felt odd, made her feel manly.

"How is he?" asked Ghada.

Mike shook his shaggy head, though his cheer diminished only a little. "Not so good," he said. "He's been real down since you called up. He'll be glad to see you. I think you'll be glad you came in time. Are you tired? I can take you up now, if you want. I can carry you both, if you don't mind crowding."

Ghada nodded. "We should go." They ate their bananas there in the store while Mike talked about the weather and asked Sabiha about Yemen.

"Are you staying long?" he asked them. When Ghada shook her head, he nodded sagely.

"It's maybe for the best," he said. "People here, not everybody's so welcoming to white folks."

Sabiha let out a shy laugh. She'd never quite imagined herself as white.

The snowmobile was sleek and alien, like a black-shelled bug, and it roared so loud that Mike had to shout to be heard over the engine, which seemed to suit him just fine.

"Your granddad doesn't come down much," he called over the engine and the crunchy scrabbling of the treads. "Never, now. I take his groceries maybe once every couple of weeks, that seems to do him. He doesn't bother nobody, and nobody's unkind to him. They think he's a little nuts, of course. In town they just call him the Mad Arab. I hope that's not offensive."

Neither woman spoke up over the engine, so after a minute of silence, he saw fit to continue.

"Can't say I blame them," Mike shouted. "The Old Town got washed away in a flood, years on years ago. I was just a kid. I barely remember it. But lots of us didn't make it. I was in my bed, and it was like a big wet hand with a thousand fingers come up out of the deep, fell over us. *Wham!* Took everything. The houses, the boats. All but one little house, a shack, my old uncle's shack. Wasn't even the highest building. It's down by the sea. There were houses up on the rock, it took 'em right off. My uncle's house, it flooded clear up to the roof, but it didn't wash up. Didn't break away. Good foundations, they said. So anyway, that's where your granddad lives now. Maybe just waiting to get washed away his own self. Why would a man do that? It don't make sense. It's mad. So we call him the Mad Arab. We don't mean anything by it."

Sabiha nodded as they slowed over poorer terrain, and felt bold enough, now, to shout herself.

"Why do you do it?" she asked. "Why do you let him squat up there?"

"He pays for his food," shouted Mike. "He's got money. But I guess— it's important to him, is all. Whatever reason he came up here, whatever he got away from, it's gotta be the most important thing in the world. I can respect that."

"We don't know, either," said Ghada—though Sabiha knew, of course. "He's crazy to us, too."

"My uncle died," said Mike, "saving the kids from that flood. The government—Indian Affairs, it was called back then—you know what his kids got? Bugger. They got bugger. 'Cause his house, that piece of shit house your granddad's in, that house is still standing." He swallowed hard. "So whatever fool thing's important to him, I respect it, even if I don't understand. I guess I wish, maybe one time, somebody'd respected what was important to me."

"That's why you bring him chicken and oranges."

"He does pay," said Mike. "But yeah. That's why."

At the end of the world, there was a rocky promontory, not very high above the sea, and on that promontory there was a small wooden house. Mike stopped well back from the house, as he always did unless there was something heavy to carry.

"I'll let you go here," he said. "Give the old man my best. I'll come back for you when that storm's run its course." He gestured toward the black sky, toward the billion trillion stars hanging suspended over the house, toward some phantom storm that the women could not see. Sabiha knew, then, that this smiling grocery-man was one who knew, too, though perhaps not in the same way. He was the only the second man she had met, after Great-Grandfather, who did.

"Come on," said Ghada. "I've been awake so long, I just want to lie on a bed. And if Great-Grandfather is in it, I'll roll him on the floor."

Great-Grandfather's face was as hollow as an old drum, and the skin stretched hard across its surface was just as dry. He'd been handsome enough once, for a spry man of ninety, with cheeks full of joy in spite of the spectral black depths of his eyes. But a monstrous war against time had been fought on that face; great trenches were dug in the slope of his forehead, and his cheeks and the flesh beneath his sunken eyes had been driven off the field. His teeth, too, those monuments of an ancient time, had been smashed and thrown down like the toppled white idols of the gods of the vanquished. Only his tremendous and sagely nose stood victorious against time; where it had once merely dominated his lean features with its aggressive presence, there was now no scrap of terrain left in that face of ages that it did not seem to command.

He opened the door with his left hand and greeted them with his right. Sabiha was tall enough now to kiss his forehead, and lowered her veil to do so out of respect. The cold of the perpetual night stung her cheeks immediately; he seemed to sense her discomfort and waved her inside.

The house was little more than a cabin, heated and somewhat lit by a wood stove. Someone, perhaps him, had put in a handful of electric lights, but the generator beside the old shack was silent as death. There was a crate of oranges on the table—no doubt a luxury here—surrounded by a heap of dried peels. Sabiha knew without asking they were all he had been eating.

They exchanged their pleasantries; and true to her word, Ghada stripped off her outer layers even as she spoke to him. His bed was a simple box-spring and mattress by the stove, and she was curled beneath the blankets before they had finished talking.

"We've come so far," she said. "I'm not used to all this. We'll talk in the morning."

"Morning will come in nineteen days," said her grandfather, but she was already too far away in dream to acknowledge him.

"She has been tremendous," said Sabiha softly. "I had no idea. I did not know you had come so far."

Great-Grandfather took down an old wooden matchbox from a high shelf. "This is the edge of the world," he said. "I had to come here."

"You said once there were many edges of the world."

"Just so," he said. "There are edges even in the Old City. You can walk to the edge of the world from your brother's door. But I had to come here, because you had to come here."

"I don't understand," said Sabiha.

"But you think you do," said Great-Grandfather. He pulled a small bundle of dried plants from the matchbox and, gingerly opening the door to the wood stove, tossed it into the fire. Almost at once a pungent and warming scent began to fill the cabin.

"What is that?"

"It will help her dream," he said. "Come down with me to where the sea is darkest."

They left the house; Sabiha had not replaced her veil, for she was with family; but the cold did not seem to bother her for long. Indeed, as they left the house behind them and came down the slope of a barren hill, the biting air came to bother her less and less.

"It's not cold," she said, a little surprised.

"It's very cold," her Grandfather said. "But you have come through the coldness of the Earth, and this is not that. Against this, you are protected. I made sure of it."

Sabiha gently brushed the pendant beneath her abaya. "Are you cold?"

"To the bone," he said. "But you are here, and my comfort no longer matters." He gestured to a small pile of firewood stacked against the side of the cabin as they came down the hill and it passed from view. "That is my firewood, the last of it. I awoke one morning two weeks ago to find my bones are too weak, now, to swing the hatchet. You came just in time for your last lesson."

"You mean my first lesson," Sabiha said. "I have waited all my life for my first lesson."

Great-Grandfather's bright, half-toothed smile of fallen idols gleamed an eerie shade of green. At first she thought she had imagined it, and then that it was some trick of his sorcery. But he did not work in such vulgar terms; he was many things, but a magician was not one of them.

"See with your larger eyes," he said.

They had come down to a barren and rocky place, a shallow promontory of mottled stone whose edges were lapped at by the patient black waters of an eerily calm ocean. The stars that had once shone so brightly overhead had faded, now, veiled behind a curtain of shimmering light that streaked across the empty sky. Cascading ribbons of radiant green filled the sky with their power, as thunderous in their majesty as they were silent in their wordless sermon.

Sabiha's mouth drifted gently open. She breathed in sharply, as if gasping for light.

"You have begun without me," Great-Grandfather said, though his tone was gentle. "You went to Damascus, as the Servant of the Forbidden did. Where Ghada sought the sciences of this world, you looked always to the night, hoping to peer behind that most foreign of veils, to look upon the faces of those who dwell beyond the stars."

"I have waited my whole life," she breathed.

"You have not waited at all," he answered. "I warned you, as a girl, that to consign these living things to dead books is to kill them with lies, and they do not like being killed any more than you or I. And so you have wisely stayed out of the footsteps of my own great-grandfather—the footsteps that drove him first mad, and then to something worse."

"I have remembered your words always," she said. "There is no truth in any book but what we bring into it."

"And if you do not learn from books—then where does truth come from?"

"From the world," she said. "And from beyond."

"You speak of the Outsiders."

"Yes."

"We have come to their door now," said Great-Grandfather, and she saw that it was true. "You have passed through the cruelty of men, through the cruelty of the Earth itself, to the place where you had thought you might speak to infinity. And I know what you expected to find there."

She had expected to find the truth—the sort of truth that screaming babies know, the sort that short-lived men of temporal power did not. She had imagined the terrible future, the ineffable eldritch names howled faintly upon a wind that blew from stranger skies than the dumb and simple blackness of space—the wind of the very breath of the slumbering Elders in their palaces beyond the night.

That, she was sure, was the howling wind of her ancestor—the wind of forbidden truths. She was certain of it. That was always how it went, in every story she had ever heard. She might go mad, but she would learn the truth of the beyond.

"And what do you hear?"

Silence.

She stood on the doorstep of the infinite void—and nothing was there.

It seemed foolish, in that moment, utterly stupid, to imagine something in the void.

"Nothing exists in the void," she said. "That's why they call it the *void*."

Great-Grandfather nodded, and spoke the simple words it had taken his lifetime to discover:

"The Outsiders are not at home."

The cultish madness Sabiha had encountered came in many ways. Like any garden-variety death cult of the Americas, there were many who conflated death, destiny, and the divine, many who firmly believed their gods would eat them, or call the souls up from their bodies, or end them in some other grisly way. It was the way of cultish thinking to embrace this abhorrence, to long for it. There was a cultivated comfort in seeing that terrible destiny through: with her own eyes, while trying to get back to Sana'a, she had seen men immolated alive in their homes, men dead of shells or shrapnel or worse things who went out of the world with faces contorted in weird serenity. To believe in the Eldest, she knew, was to believe in a fate of unimaginable horror—but even so, there was a comfort in going to meet it. The shape of her end had long been unknowable to her—and there was a warmth, at least, in *knowing*.

But there was nothing to know in that silence.

It was somehow worse.

Great-Grandfather had lowered himself down on the rock with a sense of finality. He did not expect to stand up again.

"The rest you will discover in time," he said. "You are a smart girl. Silly things like alchemy, geomancy, numbers and ciphers and forgotten names—those are simple tricks. You can learn to palm a card, too, or escape handcuffs, if it suits you. But you are about to learn the last of what I know—and it will be your burden alone to answer the question that comes of it."

If truth does not come from books—where does truth live?

When she was thirteen, he would test her with riddles—games about lions and goats, puzzles whose answers were the moon, or the wind in the reeds.

Truth must live outside of books.

"I don't want you to die," she said, a note of human affection breaking her voice slightly. "You are still my Great-Grandfather, and I am still a girl who loves you very much."

"I'm awfully old," said Great-Grandfather.

"You've been ninety as long as I can remember," said Sabiha. "You can be ninety a while longer, I think."

If the Eldest do not lie slumbering outside the world—where do they dwell?

"I quite like being ninety," he said. "People treat you with kindness. Men of far tribes, and women of other families, are no longer frightened of you. You eat less and sleep more. It's quite nice. But no, Sabiha. You are finishing now your last lesson. You are learning your first secret. And I must be ready to die, for such things never come without payment."

Sabiha felt the cold of the Earth again, a cold against which her pendant brought little warmth. It came all at once—the coldness of the spraying ocean, the frost in the eyes of the men in the airport, the terrible chill of the wind that had come up around them suddenly, as if from nowhere—the storm that Mike had predicted, that she had forgotten entirely in the stillness of her lesson. Her face was stung by water that turned to knives of ice in the air; she tasted blood on her lips, and in that moment the shimmering beauty of the green skies seemed a sharp contrast to a world steeped in an unassailable cruelty and malevolent will.

They were here, of course.

Now.

Perhaps they always had been. Perhaps the cruelty of mankind had been the howl of the insect wind all along.

The world roared as the black sea threw up a many-fingered hand, torn suddenly from its mooring among the rocks as the screaming wind struck a change in the tide. Under the thunderous incandescence of the aurora, Sabiha saw that they had not come down so far from the cabin after all; it really was just on a low rock overlooking the ocean some distance north. She saw the darkness of the icy depths come up like a thousand-headed serpent, a lashing, writhing, living scourge that flayed the rock in a steady stream and, with the aggressive deftness of a Bara'a war dancer, plucked the little cabin off the rock as effortlessly as a child picking a berry, heaving it headlong into the sea. Sabiha had the breath to call her sister's name only once before she was whelmed, too, by a claw of ocean water that knocked her from her feet with its force and blasted the air from her lungs with its chill alone. Great-Grandfather, who had been lying prone, was spared the worst of it, but he looked up with surprise, and sadness, and no small guilt as the little house was smashed to pieces on the crags by waves fighting like wolves over scraps.

"I suppose one can live a long time," he said as Sabiha slipped away into unconsciousness, "and still not know everything."

Michael Billy knew his coastal windstorms. He could smell them coming up almost out of nowhere, and could predict them even in the dead of winter when the sky couldn't hold a cloud. But even he didn't know how bad it would be until it was tearing the shingles off his roof and knocking out the village generators with surprising ferocity. He didn't waste time in getting on the phone before the lines went down, and once the Coast Guard was on its way, he rallied his brother Shane and went out himself. In a hospital in the inlet perhaps a hundred miles down the coast, Sabiha learned that his quick action probably snatched her back from the jaws of death—and it troubled her more, now, to think what death might mean now that the whole world was a dwelling place for things that ought never to have stirred from beyond the veil of night. The howling of the wind was with her still; it had drowned out even the rotors of the air ambulance, and robbed her of sleep.

In very slow English, it was explained that the blisters on her hands and feet were from the frostbite, but they had managed to save her fingers and toes. She had ruptured an eardrum in the storm or the fall, and needed a few stitches to close the gash on her head, but after they warmed her up and stabilized her that was the worst of it.

Search and Rescue had dredged up what was left of Ghada's mangled body within the first nine hours. There was no word or sign of Great-Grandfather.

The nurses watched her recovery with hostile dark eyes. It was clear they believed she should never have been there—none of them should have. One of them even went so far as to say it: "you should've stayed in the desert." But the roar in Sabiha's ear was nearly too loud to hear it, and she was too numb with grief to care in any case.

When the time finally came, she expected the trip home to be a lonely one. Her English had improved, but it was still weak. She had booked, at great expense, an empty seat for Ghada, and she would have to break the news to Nadheer and her aging mother in person. She did not have the heart to talk about it before then. It was, until the hour she rode back to the airport through an anaemic, sleety mockery of a true snowstorm, the loneliest trip she had ever taken. The pendant over her breastbone had gone cold, for reasons she might soon understand. But there in the airport, surrounded by strangers who scrutinized her dark eyes with silent hostility, a baby began to cry—then another—and she knew she would never be alone again.

Say your farewells to your family, it said. *Then come to Damascus and look for the Signs. We have a use for you—and now you are ready.*

"Will I know your purpose?" she asked, out loud, shivering. In the terminals around her, thirty thousand travelers chased their hollow destinations in a world whose doom at the hands of those who had always been there had been traded, in silence and secrecy, for doom at the hands of those who were now come. A hiss of steam from a nearby latte machine was her only answer.

"I must know!" she wailed, beating her fist against the kiosk counter, scattering a box of straws. The babies, as if screaming in a single voice, were jolted into horrid silence. The children jumped with fright, but the grown men ignored her, hustling through the terminal with planes to catch, chasing their own ties like the tails of dogs as they went about their lives above the gathering pit. Only the women looked on her with scorn and the cruelest alarm, as if she were mad, as if she were mad mad mad.

The CTHULHUSATTVA VOW

A Universe of beings imprisoned by Reason
I vow to liberate them all

Delusions of Order and Sanity are inexhaustible
I vow to break them all

Gates to R'lyeh are without number
I vow to enter them all

Cthulhu waits there, dreaming
I vow to raise R'lyeh

EMPEROR ETERNAL

Konstantine Paradias

THE WOMAN WAS GARROTED WITH a length of hair on the gilded throne of jade, her feet kicking blindly at the banquet table, sending the fine porcelain plates crashing down. The soles of her feet pounded uselessly at the marble floor, pudgy hands grasping at the strand of wire and clutching it with all the might in her atrophied muscles. She gargled and choked on the half-chewed sweetmeats, her eyes rolling to the back of her head as the chosen executioner twisted the garrote hard enough to bite into her flesh. The executioner maintained his grip even as the hair dug into his own palms, long after the woman had voided her bowels on the throne.

The *wūshī* rushed to her side, jade bowl in hand to collect the spilt fluids; there was great potency in the bounty of the just-dead. The chosen executioner retreated behind the velvet curtains, into the Maze of Broken Mirrors, where the eunuchs would put out his eyes and singe his ear-drums with red hot pokers, thus ensuring his innocence from the act that was to follow.

The *wūshī* stirred the red-brown mess in the jade bowl with his calligraphy brush, whispering the names of the one he was beseeching: the Faceless Courtesan, the Artisan of Sorrows; surveyor of all human knowledge, secret saboteur of history. Its true name was Nyarlathotep, but the people of the Middle Country called it *Luàn pá*, the Crawling Chaos.

The *wūshī* ceased his stirring just as the flautists began a maddening piping from their high perches in the amphitheater. They were children, chosen from the ranks of the serfs to have their minds crippled by opium, taught to play the secret music of the Courts of Heaven with their Xiao flutes. Their broken, halfwit minds were the only ones able to produce the sacred frequencies that could be transmitted through the lightless depths above to soothe and lull the *Báichī huángdì*—the Idiot Emperor—into a deep slumber, thus releasing the *Luàn pá* from its omnipresent grasp.

But to find and call the *Luàn pá*, to bind the thing to their bidding, the *wūshī* needed a vessel to contain his form. A bounty of flesh, an empty mind; a crude bamboo cage made infinite and inescapable through thaumaturgic geometry. The *wūshī* had but few precious moments to complete his life's work, the result of hundreds of lives lost in service to the uncaring, idiot gods above. He moved quickly, dipping the brush into the bowl, drawing the sacred designs on the skin of the woman...

Xiàng nèixiàng wài: the inward facing outward, infinite space within, swirled across her breasts.

Yǒngyuǎn de xiànjǐng: the trap set for the gods, scrawled in tiny letters around her lips, on her eyelids and ears, across the lips of her cunt and the folds of her buttocks.

Zhī jiān de kōngjiān: the sacred geometric shapes that existed in the spaces between spaces; the names of the scared prism-shapes that contained the universe within themselves, written on her belly.

Lǎo páizi: the Old Sign, the five-pointed star. The sun of his ancestors and the Ur-Men and the Leng-beasts of Tibet that was the door and the lock to keep the *Luàn pá* trapped within the vessel until the end of days, drawn with care upon her forehead.

The trap was set. The *wūshī* inhaled, filled his lungs with the scent of burning incense. From the Maze of Broken Mirrors came the screams of the chosen executioner; his cries reduced to meaningless moaning as the eunuchs completed the task, reducing him to a base hunk of writhing meat. The *wūshī* always found these broken things unsettling to look at: dolls woven from flesh and bone, held together by inborn tenacity and human medicine, bereft of the godly spark that made them men. But their palpable agony made them ideal fuel for the ritual. They drew the *Luàn pá* to them, their misery perhaps possessing an intoxicating quality to the beast. They had learned this through centuries of failure. Through their sacrifice, their predecessors had taught them how best to bind the monstrosity.

"Ph'nlui oh'tor n'garlui ftaghn," sang the mutilated concubines, rattling the terracotta jars containing their sheared breasts.

"Wgah'nagl fhtagn ar'yumun f'the," chanted the shamed monks, their severed genitals dangling from the ends of oaken canes.

The *wūshī* felt the *Luàn pá* as it descended in the room; an evil presence, a thing so massive and alien that it summoned images of monstrous landscapes, infested with eyes. It slipped through the stained-glass roof and the gravures paused in their scenes of torment, only to scream in abject horror. It bore down on the piping children, who screamed and jumped from their perches like animals to shatter their legs against the marble floor. It touched the minds of the concubines and the eunuchs and the monks and the *wūshī*, blessing them all with unbearable visions before finally entering the body of the dead woman, its essence animating the mound of dead flesh even as it bloated it near to the point of bursting.

"Nyarlathotep" the Bloated Lady spoke its own true name, in obvious defiance of *wūshī* superstition. Its voice was like powdered glass down a man's gullet.

"With sacred geometry, I bind you. By the ancient practices of *ku*, I compel you. By the *Hēi fēng*, the black wind, I constrict your arms and legs with worms." The *wūshī* chanted, flicking the calligraphy brush, spattering the Bloated Lady's lips and eyes. "Your eyes see nothing, your lips speak nothing unless I command it," he concluded, before replacing the brush in the jade bowl.

"Little man, little man, with your brushes and your scribblings and your screaming eunuchs. You spatter me with blood and excrement and you think you have me bound? I am the *Luàn pá*, the Crawling Chaos. Jangle your bone-charms and rattle your prayer-drums all you like; I'm all for a good laugh." The Bloated Lady said, rotted food and black blood spilling down from its lips, dripping down its breasts.

"There are Mongols at our borders, *Luàn pá*. There are cowards in our armies and traitors in our court." The *wūshī* said, waving away his nausea. "We have brought you here to crush our enemies and make the Middle Kingdom strong once again."

"Should I build you a Greater Wall, little man, one to reach the heavens? Or would you wish me to spread pestilence among the Mongols? With a flick of my wrist, I could turn their horses inside out, or expel their riders into the Night Above. I could find your turncoats and replace them with my agents, who are fierce and without fear or minds to call their own. Your pale-faced courtiers I could gut and replace with automatons who would be wise and incorruptible beyond measure. Is that what you would have me do, little man?" the Bloated Lady said.

All around him, the wūshī could feel the subtle vibrations that pushed against the painstakingly-crafted seals that were intended to stop the *Luàn pá* from leaving its appointed place. Even now, the Crawling Chaos was testing its restraints but would find no escape.

"Our armies will crush the Mongols at the Yellow River. Our crossbows will tear them apart and our missiles will cull them to a paltry few hundred before they have even begun their charge. But the Middle Kingdom's strength has been diminished by the machinations of cowards and black-hearted incompetents. The Jin and the Song's petty squabbles will soon make us easy picking for the barbarians. For the Middle Kingdom to flourish once again, we need an Emperor who is truly in touch with the divine, who knows the secret workings of the Heavenly Courts."

The Bloated Lady cocked an eyebrow in consideration. Stretching out a blue-green tongue, it licked its painted lips. "You would have yourself raised to the station of Emperor, little man? You would hold the seal of office with those crooked hands and wear a silken robe over your charms and trinkets?" it guffawed, slapping its hand on the arm of the throne.

"Emperor Eternal, *Luàn pá*. I wish to be nothing less. Ever-lasting and all-knowing." The *wūshī* spoke his words of treachery. Around him, he could feel the Bloated Lady's presence as tendrils of power extended to grasp the space around it, seeking to tear at the fabric of reality inside the chamber.

Behind him, the monks and the concubines were entangled in a meaningless orgy, the ghosts of their genitals meeting together in voided union. The piping children had long since ceased their screaming. Now they danced to the rhythm of some hidden music, perhaps the secret melody of the courtesans of the Idiot Emperor. In the Maze of Broken Mirrors, the eunuchs wept and beat their fists against the shattered glass.

"And what could you offer me in return, sorcerer, for my millennia of service? What could you possibly give me that would ease the burden of being contained in this fleshly cage?" the Bloated Lady said and already her skin began to crawl and flow like molten tar, her features receding until they were nothing but boiling blackness, her eyes and mouth and tongue and teeth rising to the surface like impurities in molten silver. But the signs on its body remained unchanged. The restraints still held.

"The lands beyond the Middle Kingdom. The West and the North and South with their multitudes of barbarians. The bounties of the world and the terror of its screaming millions for you to make unto a court that would put even the Idiot Emperor's to shame," the *wūshī* said and the Bloated Lady ceased her endless shifting. The screaming and the moaning and the dancing ceased. The creature which sat on the throne was suddenly still and silent, perhaps savoring the taste of a million screaming souls on its palate.

"In exchange, I wish to be unharmed by missile or blade, and to be made young again, free from the ravages of time and disease, and for the Middle Kingdom never again to suffer the indignity of an invasion until the end of time."

The Bloated Lady's eyes travelled up its body and across its face, before finally embedding themselves in the crown of her forehead, running together into a three-lobed burning eye. Its mouth expanded against its stomach, turning into a hungry gnashing gash that ripped through the silk. Its limbs ran like honey before being enveloped by its girth. Its cunt spat out long, fleshly growths like tongues that lolled and lapped at the *wūshī*'s face, coarse like sandpaper.

"It is done, sorcerer. Leave your circle so I may anoint you," the Bloated Lady said, its voice the voice of the *wushi*'s dying mother, tiny and pleading. The *wūshī* left his circle, jade bowl still in hand, shivering in terror. The tongues shot out and grabbed him the second he had stepped out of its confines, pulling him into the Bloated Lady's gash-mouth, swallowing him whole.

There was a moment of absolute horror, as its teeth chewed into his body, reducing his flesh and bone to a fine pulp.

There was an eternity of agony as the Bloated Lady's hidden barbs plunged themselves into his brain, pumping their poisonous treasure trove of knowledge. He became a part of the *Luàn pá* at that moment, perfectly prescient and omnipotent.

Then, the trauma of his consciousness being shoved back into the confines of a body reborn in her bowels, grown from his flesh in her womb, expelled out once again across the marble floor. He needn't look at the mirror to know that he was perfect, eternal, and covered in gore. He was reborn in her image, a sorcerer supreme. Looking through his new eyes, the *wūshī* saw the whirling space around him. He saw the invisible things that laid siege to reality. He saw the children, possessed by the amorphous flautists of the *Luàn pá*.

He saw all of Time and Space as a single instance, laid out before him like a woodcut print with the Idiot Emperor babbling nonsense at its center, and knew how little he had asked for, how truly small-minded his ambitions had been. The Middle Kingdom was an insignificant speck of dust and he had trapped himself in it for eternity. He raged and cursed uselessly in his own head, gnashing his teeth at the revelation. He had been a deluded fool, too caught up in his scheming, a tiny mind that had doomed the world.

"Release me from this place. I would have the world," the Bloated Lady said. The *wūshī* obeyed, his head hung in shame. Spitting at the symbols, he spoke the chants in reverse and released the *Luàn pá*. The *wūshī* watched as it floated away from its throne, shedding the relentless tug of gravity. "I thank you, sorcerer. You have given me everything for a sliver of land. Farewell."

The Bloated Lady hovered upward, about to escape its prison, when the amber doors of the place burst open in a shower of splinters. The Mongols had come, finally, had taken Yinchuan before the blood of those slain along the banks of the Yellow River had even time to dry. They reeked of fire and terror. Their curved swords dripped with gore. The Bloated Lady cackled as it saw the little men that milled about the room, struggling to keep their horses in check even as their hair went stark-white with terror at the sight of it.

It laughed even as it plucked them from the ground and popped them in its mouth as if they were candy. But the *wūshī* knew what he had to do. There was still time. Scrambling on the ground, he scooped up what little was left from the gunk in the iron bowl. Just a drop, but it would have to do. Running to the Mongols, he grabbed one of them by the reins of his horse and spoke the words that emptied his mind. He would need a steady hand. Taking one of his arrows, the *wūshī* strapped the sliver of the bowl on the tip and handed it back to him.

"Aim for its eye. Make sure not to miss," he said and spat in the Mongol's mouth, infusing him with a shred of his knowledge, giving him a glimpse of the woodcut-print universe that was their reality. The Mongol let the arrow fly and collapsed from his saddle, his brain boiling in its skull.

The arrow flew true, vibrating as it went, following an impossible trajectory . It bent and twisted and shrieked across improbable angles. The Bloated Lady, halfway through gorging on the invaders, did not notice until it was too late. The arrow pierced through the center of its eye and embedded itself in its hosts' brain, killing it immediately, destroying its anchor in the world.

The Bloated Lady howled in outrage. Across the world, children were wracked with nightmares and seers smashed the relics of their gods. Astrologists looked at their star charts and saw no rhyme or reason. Sages and savants stared at sacred manuscripts or looked for occult terms but found them to have slipped away from their minds forever. In the depths of the oceans, the hidden lords of the world beat their chests and raked their claws across their gills in mourning. The *wūshī* watched as the *Luàn pá* ascended through the hidden dimensions, torn away from the world, restored to its place in the orbit of the Idiot Emperor's court.

When it was over, the Mongols dragged the *wūshī* out in the street, to run him through with their swords. When their blades shattered against his skin, they showered him with arrows. When those failed, he was hung from the ankles, to be sawn in half from his groin to the head, but even cold iron could not penetrate his skin. So the shamans conferred with each other and fashioned a simple knife from obsidian, with which they removed the *wūshī*'s head and organs, placing them in strongboxes that were spread out across the Middle Kingdom in places that would remain forever unmarked, lost to history.

And so the Emperor Eternal remained in the Middle Kingdom, all-knowing within its confines until the end of Time.

ANTINOMIA

Erica Ruppert

Tom set himself up outside a bodega, plaintively asking for help for his imagined daughter. There were people on the street. He was good with his story. Even now, he could talk them out of money. Asa and Terry loitered several storefronts down. The red sores on Terry's arms and hands, lasting marks of her first communion, made her begging a waste of time. Their weeping soaked through her bandages in yellow stains. No one wanted to be near that. At least she did not have the blight, with her flesh turned hard, black, and crumbling.

"Ter," Asa said into her ear. "Look who's coming."

"Wonderful," she said, and rose from her slouch against the building.

The man walking toward them was short and muscular, and carried himself like a wrestler. Terry stepped forward to meet him, motioning Asa to stay back.

"Pauly," she said.

He snorted at her. "You said you were moving on, Terry. This doesn't look like it."

Behind him, Tom was paying attention. Terry kept her eyes on Pauly. She felt a familiar pressure build inside her skull.

"We're just passing through. Not coming back."

Pauly leaned in to her, shoving his blighted fingers into her face. "Get your fucking ass out of here."

Asa reached for him but Terry raised her hand, warning him back. She pressed into Pauly and wrapped her arms around his shoulders. He flinched from the contact. Her face ran with sweat. She knew him well enough to know he was afraid of her now, afraid of her affliction. He tried to dislodge her hold on him, but she only tightened her grip. She could feel her skin heating up, knew that it was turning an ugly boiled red. The few passers-by steered well clear of them.

"Come on, Pauly," she breathed against his mouth. "Don't you remember the good times?"

Then her grip slipped, and she began to fall. Asa took her weight as Pauly broke free. Tom ran to help as Terry sagged to the broken pavement. Her mouth opened, and the voice that spilled out was a thick moan of wind. It had no words for her then, and ended in a hollow scream. Her muscles twitched. She opened her glassy eyes.

"Take me home," she said.

Pauly still stood there, gaping at her. Tom lifted her like a child and pushed past him.

When it all fell apart, Terry was ready, full of hope. She set herself up as a prophet, telling whoever would listen that she knew the way out. What after all is salvation if not escape?

She got the attention of people more lost than she had been, and led them into the empty suburbs where she could preach without distraction. She swore she spoke for the divine. But the first time it spoke through her, with her own mouth, her small group of sycophants fled. Spasms and the fever of revelation cracked her skin like brittle leather, and she bled, and she howled, and she burned. It was nothing she could have imagined.

Only Tom and Asa stayed with her, frightened and sure. They believed her and kept her safe through the pain of it. It was exactly what they had imagined.

After that, she offered no more prophecy. She would be nothing more than a vessel.

✱

Tom and Asa took turns carrying her until she was steady enough to walk. She still held their arms, her head hanging, exhausted but unable to rest. When they were clear of the populated blocks Terry stopped and sat on the curb.

"There's more coming," she said. "Can you feel it? It's like the sky is coming down on my head."

"Your skin is bad," said Asa. "Let's just get home."

She nodded and let them lead her through the crumbling streets. The slumped houses reminded her of where her parents had lived, block after block of quietly falling-down brick Capes built in a booming post-war optimism. The familiarity had drawn her out here. Years ago, she had tried to go back home. The house had been boarded up with a red cross on the door and weeds spilling out of the flowerbeds. She wondered sometimes where her family had gone. She never tried to find them. Too much had happened to her for her to go back. She replaced them, instead.

The house she had chosen for her band to squat in was still solid, though the roof did leak in places in a hard rain. Tom went in first to light a lamp and start a fire. Clouds had followed them back and the air was grey, cool, and unpleasantly damp. Terry trembled, worn out. Asa guided her to her favorite chair and wrapped a blanket around her. Beside the fire she dozed and almost dreamed. It was coming. It would be here soon. She opened her eyes and gazed into the flames.

Time drifted. She roused, saw Asa reading and Tom sprawled comfortably on the couch.

"I can't go back there," she said.

"Probably not," said Asa. "We'll manage it."

Light crept in around the drawn shades, dull yellow through the overcast. There was a tentative soft knock on the front door, and the three of them pricked up. Tom rose and slipped a gun from the waistband of his pants as Asa went to the door. He peered through the peephole into the distorted face of a young man. On the porch behind him was a thin girl.

He opened the door quickly. Tom stood beside him and raised the pistol.

"Please," the kid said. "We saw the smoke from the chimney. Can we come in?"

"Why would you want to do that?" Asa said.

The kid glanced over his shoulder at the girl. She was sinking into herself.

"It's weird out here today, there's something out here, in the air. I don't know what. Look, we have food."

The kid held out a thin nylon bag to Asa. "Here, take it. It's canned stuff." He didn't wait for Asa to examine it, but rushed on. "Look, at least just let Amy in, she won't be any trouble. Please."

Asa cocked an eyebrow at Tom.

The girl had the blight, not too badly. The rims of her nostrils were traced finely in black, and her earlobes were gone. She had been pretty, once.

Terry materialized at Tom's shoulder, quiet as a cat in the shadows. "Let them in," she said. "What have you got besides food?"

The kid looked at Tom, and then Asa, before he let his eyes settle on Terry. "Nothing," he said. "We smoked it."

Terry smiled. "Would have brought you farther."

She turned away from them and walked carefully back into the living room. Asa stepped back to let them pass.

Terry returned to the low chair near the fire, and she motioned Amy to sit by her. The kid hovered after her.

"Who are you?" Terry asked, waving him back.

"John," he said.

"Of course. And she is Amy, you said. And you are afraid of the dark."

John shrugged, uneasy.

"There's something big out there, like a storm coming down."

Terry paused for a moment, then turned to the girl. "Do you feel it, too?"

Amy shook her head and let her hair fall over her face.

"Look, she can't talk, alright?" John said. "Let me sit by her."

"Why can't she talk?" said Tom.

"Blight," John said. "Her tongue's gone."

Terry picked at her bandaged hands.

"Something gets us all," she said.

They all fell silent. The fire popped.

"We saw you in town," John said. "We saw you. Saw it come over you. It's like that for Amy, too. It comes on her like that."

"Really?" said Asa from the doorway. "Just like that?"

John looked up at him, confused and wary. Terry watched him begin to figure it out, and nodded her head. Tom stepped up to John and pulled the trigger. The shot was huge in the small room, flat and ugly. Tom fired again, and John collapsed like a broken wheel.

Echoes hung over them for a few bleak seconds before Amy opened her black-stained mouth and shrieked. The girl lunged forward but Terry grabbed her and held onto her. Amy's cry fluted up from shrill to musical, and her body heaved with sobs.

"Like a bird," Terry said, wonder in her voice. "Listen to her."

Suddenly Amy convulsed, her spine cracking as she writhed. Her eyes rolled back under fluttering lids and her cries decayed to grunting. She twisted out of Terry's grasp and fell heavily to the floor. Terry stepped back, almost into the fire. Amy rolled, and her thrashing hands clawed and locked around Terry's ankle.

"Get her out of here," Terry said, kicking free.

Amy grew quiet where she lay, her breath coming in long gulps. Tom and Asa bundled her up and carried her to the back of the house.

Terry leaned over to see what was left of John. The carpet beneath him was sodden. She wouldn't look at his face.

"This next," she called out. Then it was on her.

It spoke through her as a low rumble, a darkness come like storm clouds rolling up from the horizon. Her vision filled with thick golden light, blinding her. Tom and Asa came back into the room but she couldn't see them, only their thin shadows against the sudden heavy glare. They saw the sheen in her eyes and grabbed her, held her up as her head rolled back and her legs shook and faltered. She could not hear them anymore, could barely feel their hands on her where they gripped.

Image faded into image, light into light. She saw the ghosts of everything. It was in her.

Then like a wave it passed. She shrugged away from Tom's lingering hold, wiped the loose spit off her mouth with the back of her hand. Her legs gave out and she sat heavily before Tom could steady her. She waved him off.

"I need water," she said. "It hurts."

"There's a pool down the block that has water in it, knee deep at least. We could use that," Asa said.

"Now," Terry said, her skin flushed red and already beginning to peel. The two men carried her across the dry ragged lawns to the lonely back yard. The pool was above ground. Asa climbed into the tea-colored water, his feet kicking up slick leaves from the bottom. He braced himself to take her weight as Tom lifted her over the side. She was burning. Her skin shredded away under his hands, curls of it floating on the autumn air.

Tom clambered in and together they lowered her into the cold brown water. She cried out as her head began to slip under, then shut her mouth and eyes and let it take her. Under the surface she opened her mouth to let the water in, to let it cool her fire. Although she held her breath it filled her throat with a bitter taste like tobacco. She opened her eyes, then, and suddenly missed the air. Her back arched in panic.

Tom and Asa each took an arm and pulled her up to sit. They knelt beside her as she coughed and swallowed air. She wiped flecks of leaves from her stinging eyes and looked up into the steely sky.

"Let me rest," she said, slurring. Her head fell forward and she was gone.

She woke with a start and struggled free of the blankets wrapped tightly around her. Asa stroked her cheeks as she calmed down. She realized she was on the back porch of the house. There was still daylight. She got to her feet and held on to the bare railing.

"Where is Amy?" she said.

Asa pointed to a shrouded figure stretched on the ground.

"I don't know what happened," he said. "It looked like a fit. She stopped breathing. She never came out of it."

Terry swayed where she stood, finding her balance.

"This is bad," she said.

Asa put his arms around her.

"She had the blight. It was probably worse than it looked. We couldn't have known."

Terry pulled away from him.

"No," she said, her voice tight. "It wasn't the blight. This is bad. He spoke through her like he speaks through me. This is so bad."

She knelt next to Amy's body and tugged back the sheet. Amy's face was dark, the skin puffed and seamed like lava.

"She couldn't bear it. She was too weak," Asa said. "Not you."

"We have to leave here," Terry said. "It isn't clean here anymore."

Asa looked at her evenly.

"He follows you," he said.

Terry threw the sheet back over Amy's face and got to her feet. She could feel the pressure building behind her eyes. Her cheeks warmed, and she blotted at her mouth with the damp bandages on her wrist. "Where's Tom?"

"Over in the next block digging a grave."

"I have to see," she said, and stumbled toward the front of the house. Asa began to follow her.

"No," she said. "Stay with Amy."

Terry made her way to the street and slowly across it to the front steps of the house there. She sat down, dizzy and exhausted. Her head was full of lightning. Her skin burned from within, and she peeled off the bandages covering her hands and arms. Steam vented from the sores. This was it, now, this was her turn to carry it.

Her scalp pricked, and she squinted up to the sky. Fire rained down, in threads and droplets. The air sparkled. She stood and raised her arms into it, turned her face up to the flames. Her hair smoked where the fire landed. She opened her mouth to it. She worshipped, uncertain, afraid.

Darkness stirred.

The clouds were black, now, and roiled in her head. She could not see, the light would not come. Tom and Asa were gone from her. She was somewhere they could not follow.

The rumble rose to a roar, the voice made of thunder and wind and the crash of waves. It was coming, through her, its promise filled. Her skin burned, scattered like ashes. Her flesh smoldered, exposed.

Her heart flinched away.

She was not ready.

FEEDING the ABYSS

Rhoads Brazos

HER FIRST DAY ON THE JOB, TWO numbing weeks after Gerald left
with a shrug, she arrived at the front gate of the Willow Gables, a gated
community for the well-to-do, its every rolling acre dotted with mini-
mansion and guest house pairs. Her waiting partner was an older Asian
fellow with short iron-gray hair and a black suit of modest means that
didn't hide the swell of his waist. Clearly, his height served as an excuse.
She favored the same tactic herself. He noticed her approaching from
a retreating cab and crushed his cigarette under the toe of a scuffed
wingtip boot.

"Ms. Bird?" he asked.

"Lily's fine," she said.

"Daisuke. My friends call me Dice." He gave her a quick head to toe
appraisal, lingering upon the tattoos peeking from under her sleeves
but saying nothing. For that she was thankful. She needed the job.
Not having Gerald at the apartment made rent day iffy.

"They told you?" she asked.

Only after the agency had checked her qualifications—do you have
a driver's license?—and made their offer, did she mention she was

female. Over the phone, it wasn't always obvious. Her voice was husky, she flattered herself.

"Oh, I've known for a while. So," he said, "no championship ring?"

She'd signed her application L. Bird.

"They wouldn't take me seriously," she said. "You understand?"

He grunted. "Sister, we do what we must, but I should warn you—"

"Please don't coddle me."

He cut his words short with a smirk. "Hop in. I'll do the talking. Your job is to not look surprised."

She took a seat in the front of the transport van, and Dice explained between sips of coffee what she needed to know. Depressed widower, alone for years. He'd been lying in his bedroom most of the month before anyone deigned to look in.

Dice tossed her a paper mask. "Gloves are in the box. Breathe through your mouth. And remember, *cargo*. Always call them cargo."

In the house, she slipped the bag under the dead man while Dice guided in the feet. The body was as green as a frog, hopping with life not its own. It lay in a nest of pornography: every shade of sweating flesh, greasy angles and fluids, crotch shots and lips in feigned *O*s of satisfaction, matching the deceased in ways those glossy girls couldn't have imagined.

Dice pulled a remote from the guy's fingers and zipped the bag. Together, they lifted the corpse onto the stretcher. Dice signed off with a seedy junior detective who had been watching their progress with a creepy nonchalance. Every time Lily found his eye, it was either on her ass or crawling over the porn.

As they hoisted their load onto the van's lift, Dice apologized. "They seldom go with dignity."

She'd prepared a witty response, but couldn't bring herself to say it.

"You okay?" he asked.

She nodded.

"You're doing great. Next one will be easier."

It wasn't. The girl had died at her dorm room keyboard, her skin a glowing gold, her hair in a spill of copper. She was posed like sculpture, like a sighing angel stretched over a marble tomb. In high school, Lily had prayed for this look.

The police had left the computer on. "For the forensics guys," Dice explained. The goodbye note still showed. The machine chirped and by reflex Lily read the incoming message: *It's Mom, please call.*

She thought she had it under control at the next stop, a hairpin curve overlooking a golf course. The victim had met the asphalt face first, so she couldn't focus her imagination. Under the strobes from a dozen police cruisers, she and Dice gathered the body and fed it into the van.

"One more and we're at capacity," Dice said and tossed her a bag. "You do it."

"Me? I—"

"She's light." He motioned to the wreckage, a late-model sedan wrapped around a broad elm, a flowered cross already nailed in place. It confused Lily at first, as if the police would bother with such a courtesy, until she noticed the tree's scarred base.

She didn't see anyone in the passenger's spot. "Where?"

"In back." Dice lit a cigarette and turned away. "Car seat."

Lily stood rooted to the spot. Her pulse hammered with each flash of red and cooled on blue. The job was about more than money. She'd lost everything and come here to hide. She wanted the task of an outcast, to crutch her solitude upon an excuse. She knew a lot about excuses.

When Dice mumbled tepid encouragement, she stomped away. The police kept their attention locked on her expression, forcibly placid. Could they see though her mask? Could they read her like any other suspect?

I'm a fake. I'm pretending. I'm afraid.

The car's front window was folded in like a tangle of cobwebs, the ceiling crunched down so low Lily had to climb inside at a stoop. She fumbled with the bag's zipper and somehow opened it before letting it slip from her fingers. Someone spoke over her shoulder. A woman's voice, maybe? Such an odd accent. It told her to stay distant, and that was good advice. She could see its logic.

She took the child in her arms. The little girl looked to be sleeping, and so Lily pretended she must be. This soul had never experienced life, or maybe she had, the only part worth knowing. It was good she'd left early. With every year it diminished. But that was her own neuroses speaking again, wasn't it? Excuses, and not for this child.

Dice took the bundle from her arms. "Use gloves next time."

"She's clean."

"Never presume."

Lily walked to the front cab and climbed in. She buried her face in her hands and wept.

They drove into the early morning hours. The sky behind them shone a suburbial yellow-gray. Ahead, it stretched as a slab of slate. Twice, Dice stopped the van and went stumbling through the darkened ditch like a souse. It seemed odd to Lily, and she thought he might have some unspoken medical issue. When he rejoined her, they drove with the radio off.

"Not many people appreciate this job," he said after a particularly long stretch of quiet. "But it's important. You want to talk?"

"Not right now."

He gave her a sideways glance. "We need to."

She stared out the side window. This far from the city, she could make out the stars like pinpricks of static. They fell in strange patterns, constellations she'd never seen in books.

"You're a natural," Dice said. "I can tell."

"I'm a liar."

"We all are, in chosen ways. Twenty years ago I told my wife I was cheating on her. She slapped me so hard my teeth still rattle. What she didn't know, and could never guess, was that I made it all up." He turned from the main road onto a graveled path of poor repair. When it faded to nothing, he continued on a bouncing course through a field of stubble. "You look as surprised as she did."

"Now why would you do such a thing?"

"The usual reason. She was stifling me. This is it."

Dice stopped the van stopped, let it idle.

"We'll do it here," Dice said.

"If you think I'm going to screw a guy old enough to be my father in a truck full of corpses—"

He laughed. "Cargo, call them cargo."

"I'm not afraid of you."

He seemed particularly delighted at this pronouncement. "*Subarashii!* I know, I'm too old for you. Now come help me. I was in a hurry once and got the wheels stuck. That's never good. You saw the flashlight in the glove box?"

In the glow of her beam, he did a slow circuit of the area, all the while muttering under his breath. Lily followed with more irritation than fear. He wheezed too much to raise concern.

After retracing their path, Dice hopped back in the driver's seat. Lily joined him and they began a slow loop.

"Turn around," Lily said.

"Always counterclockwise, remember that."

"You know what I mean. To town."

Dice cracked his window and sniffed the air. "You could have driven off. I left the keys. So why didn't you?" When she didn't answer, he continued. "A touch inquisitive, I think. And maybe you already know who wants to visit? You're a natural, as I said. Fate brought us together."

Lily smelled smoke. It didn't seem to be from the van. It wasn't the acrid stink of oil and scorched rubber, but charred bone, burning hair, an eyeless brood squirming on a funeral pyre.

"You are so blessed?" Dice gave her a searching look. "You sense her. I can tell."

The dome of the night sky was a vast pupil of black rimmed with an iris of stars. Lily squeezed her knees tight. The area they'd paced out had soundlessly fallen away. The van circled a pit.

"I've seen this," she whispered, and gasped at the realization of her own words.

"In dreams, yes, go on."

"Before coming down, vultures circle the dead. We're letting the dead circle the vultures. That calls them up?"

"Her."

A name like corrosion burned Lily's tongue. When she struggled to shape its syllables, her lips went numb.

There was a hiss, a crack like a thunderbolt, and then it was there, towering, reaching from the hells to the heavens. A magnificent column of smoke and eyes and teeth. It was a gullet into a core of nothingness. It, she, chewed the air.

A voice whispered at Lily's shoulder, feminine with a peculiar accent.

Look into me, little one.

Somewhere, someone was screaming.

A hand gripped her by the left shoulder, shook. Dice spoke in a raspy baritone over the stink of nicotine but—Daisuke, he called himself?— that was a lie.

Lily opened her eyes. "You're not even a man."

Dice showed a flash of surprise. The rise of a smile crossed his lips, but disappeared as the van shook and shuddered. His coffee spilled over the dash. He slammed on the brakes.

"Listen to me!" he cried.

A blur cracked against the window and starred the glass outward. Dice saw the damage and swore.

"Have faith," he said, "and she will treat you as a daughter, as one of the thousand. Do not fear! The cargo—" He pressed his hands over his ears. "It's all hers! If she gets less than four she'll tear you to pieces. Choose three."

Outside, madness descended in a jet-engine roar of lunacy, a cyclone of tears and laughter riding a razor-edge agony. The spire of the pit was a mother, a queen, a goddess. To debase herself by entering existence, it brought her shame. If she wasn't sated—

The driver side door flew open and Dice jumped out. He turned back to Lily and held up four fingers, then three. He raced into the fray, shouting.

"Make me new! Iä! Shub-Niggurath! Make me—"

Tendrils swept him into the sky. There was a piercing cry and the splintering of bone. Viscera rained down.

What had he done? Lily fought to breathe. The van lurched upward and slammed back to earth with enough force to drive her into the ceiling. It wasn't about to wait. If she cowered, she was dead.

The gale wrenched the door from her grasp. She fell to the cold earth and crawled like a blind insect. Grit and debris blasted into her, but somehow she staggered to her feet and opened the back of the van. There wasn't time to use the lift. She pulled the nearest tray and closed her grip on a moist thigh. She knew which body she had but didn't falter. She slipped an arm under its back, wrapped it in a bear hug, and hoisted the corpse teetering to its feet. Whatever filth was dribbling from the jaw and soaking her front went ignored.

With an effort that threatened to tear ligament from bone, she spun and launched two-hundred and fifty pounds of stale widower skyward.

The goddess plucked the cold flesh from the air. For two heartbeats the dead man floated, and then was shredded like a squirrel in a woodchipper. A thousand mouths swallowed it all down. Lily didn't wait. She dragged Roadkill Dad out by the ankles and spun again, released the body like an Olympic hammer throw, launched it ten yards at least. He never hit the ground.

Three, Dice had said, and she thought she understood. He counted himself as one, so that left a choice, didn't it? Another dire test, like back at the accident, to see how she'd cope. She felt the goddess watching with cold amusement. To spoil the ritual earned a penalty of the worst sort.

The decision was easy, really. You just had to stay distant.

Lily gathered the bundle from the last tray. So light. A proper sacrifice should hurt the most. Any less would be an insult. When she turned and made to whisper an apology, the child's body was torn from her fingers. Gone, and yet she could hear something. Something of what the girl had used to be was keening.

Screaming. Lily could hear all of them, screaming an agony usurping death. It had no end. They were lost upon the winds of Sheol.

She slumped to the ground and hid her face.

The din mounted around her. The being pushed close and extended cold tendrils, to within inches of her face. One touch and she would be fodder. One brush and her frail body would erupt into corruption. And from within a fury of ecstasy and fever, the goddess spoke.

I know you're here.

Lily sobbed. That was all she had ever wanted.

She spent the next hours on the interstate loop skirting the city. It wasn't easy keeping the vehicle in its lane; her mind wandered. At dawn a knock sounded from the van's back partition, very like the sound she'd dreaded to hear when she'd started off last evening. She'd been imagining those bodies opening their eyes or grabbing her hand.

The knock came again, shave and a haircut. She whispered a *thank you* and pulled into a truck stop.

She parked alongside the diesel pumps and opened the back. The college girl cargo hopped out. It stood barefoot on the asphalt and studied its arms and waist. It—*she*—seemed pleased.

"What do I call you now?" Lily asked.

"Dice still works," the girl said, and gingerly touched her ears. She frowned at the number of piercings. "Nicely neutral, has a kind of swagger, don't you think?"

"Why four?"

"You're not going to ask about—"

"Why not six?"

"Don't be so Hollywood. Four is totally unlucky. Death, four, *shi*. That's in my old tongue." She gave a sour expression. "God help me, this girl has nothing to offer. A bit of casual French? *Parles-tu anglais?* Ghastly. But I can text with the best of them now." She raised an eyebrow. "You're taking this in stride."

Lily studied her hands, palms up. Her fingers trembled. She squeezed them into fists.

"Ah, yeah. That," Dice said. "I saw it all, you know. You knelt at the altar. That's such an honor. Just be glad she didn't say anything. Her words would have left you hollow."

Lily spoke softly. "The empty vessel holds a wind from between the stars."

"A natural. When I first saw you, I knew."

A big rig approached in a hiss and rumble. The driver gave them both a strange look of concern. They must be quite a sight, Lily caked in gore and Dice primping her hair behind a cadaver transport.

"Can I crash at your place?" Dice winced at her own words. "Excuse my lingo. It takes, like, weeks to find your old voice. It's just that I forgot my keys in my pocket, in my old suit, or whatever. My landlord won't be cool with this."

Lily agreed. She needed answers. It would be best if Dice stayed near.

The next day, they broke into Dice's eastside flat and took everything of value, oil paintings of ballroom couples and of women shaded under peacock plumes, bundles of scrapbooks, and antique whatnots. While they packed the van, Dice grumbled about losing her deposit. She made herself at home at Lily's apartment, and when weeks turned to months, moved from the couch to the daybed in Gerald's old office.

They often sat over a dinner of *sashimi* and *udon* and discussed reality. Dice spoke of colossal intelligences drifting through interstellar gulfs; of humanity, a sinking ship which only the boldest souls abandoned to tread a bottomless ocean. The one question Lily never asked was *why*? Why had Dice, centuries ago, dedicated herself to this task? The answer couldn't be more obvious, for it guided her too. In a world of limitations, only a fool would hesitate to touch the infinite.

Dice had confessed that the agency was a ruse of her own invention. For a week, she'd paid her out-of-work neighbor to screen calls. What she wanted is what she found: the rare female who shared her passion. She was in this alone, or she had been, she had said with a smile, then scooted close.

On their jaunts, they went where inspiration took them, following, as Dice called it, the *carnal charnel*, the perfume of their mistress. They could sniff out a body with unerring accuracy. A homeless woman frozen under the I-22 overpass. The back alley remains of a junkie runaway. A jogger with a heart condition, still sheened in sweat. No one ever interfered. Coincidence conspired on their behalf.

The police were surprised to be met by a woman as butch as a prizefighter and an oddly confident sorority girl, but not every brow was raised. Morgue-bound bodies didn't disappear without consequence. Someone had to be meddling with the paperwork, and as Dice pointed out, that proved they weren't alone. Shub-Niggurath spread the seeds of insight. She birthed a thousand young.

In such ways, they gathered their cargo county-wide. Dice sought out the point of contact, always in a remote location, and Lily learned to feel it too. It came as a taste like rotted meat dipped in honey, or as an itch tickling deep in her neck, as if an insect were climbing her throat. They circled with the van until the goddess arose in her awful splendor.

Victims and aggressors, proud debutantes and common street whores, feeble old men and teenage immortals. Oh, how she could eat! She chewed them into dust. Lily imagined how surprised they must be. What must their moment of new awakening be like? To be resurrected in Shub-Niggurath only to live forever, screaming within the bones of eternity.

Though she held Dice as a dear friend, and didn't shy away from her casual touches, she didn't share everything with her. When the goddess whispered, she listened with measured breaths. Those rare words were only meant for her.

One summer night on the outskirts of a disused airfield, she risked it all. While Dice offloaded an easily manageable cargo, Lily crawled to the roaring threshold. On all fours, she dared a plea, one which she'd never allowed to cross her lips.

"Mother, help me."

She didn't explain further. She didn't need to. The whole universe knew her failure.

A flurry of images pressed in. She saw slug-bodied monstrosities below the deepest sea beds, drinking the oceans. She wandered across cities rotting into black putrescence. She crawled naked over a breathing soil that hungered to swallow her down. When she turned her face to the heavens, the sky opened and comets fell like hailstones. To show the scope of true catastrophe, was that the intent? Her concerns were less than nothing when framed against the cosmic. She felt tears welling and then the goddess spoke.

Take him back.

Lily gathered herself on the front step of a postwar rental, a boxy relic done in beige with pastel trim. The screen door was caved in like a hammock. The neighbor's dog wouldn't stop barking. She knocked.

From inside came the sounds of reality TV. Censored bleeps and orchestral swells gave it away. Gerald had done nothing but deride television back when they'd been together. Lily listened for details, something she could use in later conversation.

The door creaked open and Gerald appeared in a wrinkled T and saggy shorts. His forehead only came to her nose, his glasses needed cleaning. He seemed thinner, less there, as if their time apart had drained him. He blinked against the sun.

"Jesus, Lily." He shifted uneasily. "I thought we agreed."

"Yeah, I know. I wanted—"

He only met her eye for an instant. His own always found somewhere else to be.

"Just listen," she said. "Things have happened. Things, to me... I want to say. I'm sorry, I mean. I want to say that."

He gave a light laugh, meant to be disarming.

"I like your place." She waited for him to brag. When the moment stretched long, she added, "You shaved."

"It itched. It always did."

"You look nice."

A lie. He had a weak chin.

He gave a half shrug and took a step back.

"Wait," she said, more emphatically than she'd meant.

He wanted to be anywhere but here, she could tell. This wasn't how it was supposed to happen. In her imaginings, at this point they'd already been hugging; they'd forgiven each other and all their pointless mistakes. Yet she could salvage it. Focus was the key. She needed to be confident but not overbearing. Vulnerable, but not helpless. Somehow sexy, but not a whore. That's what a guy wanted.

It was fucking impossible.

"Let's just catch up," she said. "I found some things of yours back at the place and got to thinking, that's all. Maybe we can go out for coffee?"

"You drink now?"

Too desperate. Her cheeks burned. "Sure. I saw a cafe down the block."

"It's not very good."

"Oh, I—"

"Listen," he said, and she remembered their final day. Incompatible, he'd said then, he said now. Not her fault or his. Theirs. They'd had moments he would always cherish, and he hoped she would too, but it was time to move on.

"Nothing's forever," he said.

"That's not true at all. I've seen it. I've felt it."

He looked at her quietly. "Don't come back, please?"

"Can I—" The door swung shut.

On the walk back to the van, her spirit spun in the muck of old memories: junior prom rejections, first dates that never led to a second. Through it all, her painted-on smile. She lifted her head, expecting an accusing scowl from Dice, but she was in the driver's seat fiddling with her phone. An old habit, a new vice. When Lily climbed up and in, Dice gave her hand a squeeze.

They drove back to the apartment and Lily cried in the bathroom until she felt cleansed. She busied herself straightening. She mucked about the kitchen and then gathered Gerald's things—old magazines, a set of keys she didn't recognize, a small collection of DVDs, mostly B-movie fare featuring firearms and alien invaders. The bottom case had a mismatched disk, his attempt at subterfuge. She popped it into her laptop, not for the first time, and watched with the sound down low.

Is this what he'd wanted? Permissive flesh, debased longing, or was it just a guy thing? The women didn't look anything like her. Another rejection of sorts, she supposed. She watched and considered.

Dice's voice came from behind. "I wasn't going to say anything."

Lily snapped the laptop shut. "Then don't."

"Have some dignity."

"You should talk. Weren't you in one?"

"It was the seventies. I was feeling down. But that's not what I meant." She motioned to the tray cooling on the oven. Stacked upon it were a dozen rhubarb-jellied cookies. "His favorite?"

Lily scowled.

"I understand," Dice said. "You can only feel so much pain in a lifetime, right? Well, I'm over the limit. I'm an expert in loss. You find someone you want to be with and then they can't be bothered to let you in. I've lived it enough times. I'm living it now."

Lily spun and marched out of the kitchen, cutting short an uncomfortable confession.

"Please." Dice hurried after her. "This is important. You need to know. I—"

"She told me to."

Dice knew who Lily meant. She searched her face for a trace of jest, measuring the consequences of risking such a lie against the impossibility that it was true.

"She said I could have him. We're meant to be together."

"Him? You mean *Gerald*? By name?"

"No, but when I asked—"

"So you two chatted over tea?" Dice laughed. "Your words would be lost in the maelstrom, along with your mind."

Lily argued against it. She described the voice of Shub-Niggurath, shivering on the air like a flute over a choir of brass.

"And we already hear her," she said. "She tells us where to go."

"That's not the same and you know it. The wind of fate carries her purpose."

"Not true. She whispers."

"She does not speak to you!"

Dice trembled, or the body she'd taken did.

Those hazel eyes weren't hers, even if they did flash with her anger. Those lips, pressed into a curt frown, belonged to another. Lily saw through her veneer down to her ancient core, a soul which on the occasions she'd asked, couldn't even remember its many names. Yes, she had let Dice near, and one tipsy night had even allowed her to kiss her fingertips, but she could never be with someone who wore their skin like drapery.

All that remained was the truth.

"You're jealous," she said.

"*Baka-chan!* It's in your head. Do you understand?" Dice grabbed her hands. "It's not her. It's you."

Lily wrenched herself away. The motion sent Dice sprawling to the floor. She sat slumped upon her knees, her back curved like a question mark.

"You think I don't know?" She rasped like an old crone, which she was. "You're running out of time."

"Stop it."

"Ah, so you do follow? Well there are other ways to be a mother. Once, I—"

"Get out!"

Dice blinked rapidly. She made to protest but couldn't form words.

Lily yanked her to her feet and dragged her squirming toward the front door. Amid vows of how much she was needed, she shoved Dice out onto the landing.

"Please," Dice managed, and Lily slammed the door in her face.

The apartment seemed to be holding its breath. The creak and thump of the neighbors' movements had stilled. This shame too, the whole world knew.

After a few buzzing moments, footfalls receded down the steps. From the balcony window, Lily watched the van ease down the street. It made a left at the corner and was gone.

How was it fair? She didn't feel what Dice did and couldn't fake an honest return, and so she'd dismissed the only person who understood her. If only Gerald could intuit half as much. He'd used her as a temporary comfort. He shut the door on her just this morning. When love was professed, he ran away.

She was just like him.

She spent her days on the couch with the front door unlocked. Maybe when Dice came by for her things she would see it as symbolic. Lily waited.

The hum of traffic swelled throughout the day. In the early morning and evening, the jouncing clatter of heavy trucks joined in. Vaguely, she thought of chores and buying groceries. She emptied the wallets she and Dice had gathered onto the kitchen table. There was so little cash left, and she didn't dare touch the credit cards. She still had a shoebox full of jewelry, cell phones, and collected odds and ends, but was wary of the attention she'd draw pawning it.

Twice on clear nights, the pull of the goddess directed her to dying souls, and twice she hid under the blankets. She begged forgiveness and explained how she couldn't possible manage, and the feeling faded.

On a rainy Saturday evening, it came again, and she began her usual entreaties. This time the feeling didn't lessen, but clenched her all the tighter. She wept excuses and it redoubled. It punched at her gut, driving her breath out in a great whoosh. Her head filled with the scent of lavender and decay. She could taste the fumes upon the air, leading to the door and away, down to the street to the old folks' lodge, then miles across town to a backyard swimming pool, cutting back to the suburbs inside a smoky garage, bring a mask, over again—

"*No no no no no,*" she begged, and the visions faded.

The room tilted. She slid up the wall in a rough tumble. The furniture didn't move, just her and whatever she happened to knock loose. Hanging pictures flew to the floor, now the ceiling. Blows pounded down, cracking her bones like a thousand hammers.

She screamed and writhed through the agony until she could take no more. She croaked a single word: "Mercy."

She lay gasping upon the ceiling and collected herself. She struggled to her knees and rubbed at her stinging eyes. Up had become down, and down up, but only for her. The world went on without notice. This was a miracle, an alien gravity, and more. A punishment? No, proof.

"But I already believe," she said. She crouched quietly.

The living room shadows shifted. She squinted through drying tears. Something was here, not the goddess, but another form, a massive bulk standing upon elephantine legs and wavering long tendrils toward the carpeted floor above. It obeyed the same gravity she did.

She let her mind search through hidden ways. "You're of Sheol," she finally said. "A Child?"

The mouth atop its head, wide enough to walk into, linked its teeth together into a grin that swallowed the couch. All these days, she'd been sleeping inside it.

It was an eyeless thing, yet it saw her, she knew. It reached for her with a single long tentacle. She shrank away. When the appendage showed no malice, she took it with tentative fingers. It led her by the hand down the wall and to the floor, where she stood upright again.

Then the creature was gone, and impossibly, she felt the pang of loss.

"Wait," she said. "Don't—"

It stood next to her. Its tentacles coiled over the carpeting and disappeared through the walls. It could only be seen from an odd angle when the eye sought a particular light. How could she not have noticed it before? It had been here all week, all year, her entire life. When she was a child, lying under a garish cartoon bedspread, she hadn't been alone. She'd imagined the dark corners of the room were watching her, and they had been. They'd been told to.

What a fool she'd been! To hear and run away. She deserved to be consumed, but Shub-Niggurath had blessed her instead. As a mother herself, this one sin she forgave. Lily's penance was spent in the belly of a whale, its mouth its womb. She'd lain fetal and shared its essence, hers, and gestated into a new being. Now, spit upon the shore, she wouldn't hesitate to act.

"Can you hear me, I wonder?" she asked. "I'll wait and speak to you on the threshold. But I know. I don't need another answer, because you've already said. You want what I want because it's not selfish at all."

She breathed in life. With each inhale it filled her—her neighbors, and their neighbors, the people down the block, surrounding traffic, couples in restaurants. She felt their remaining days as a pressure, the swell of a person's presence against the hollow of their absence, the gap between them electric.

She settled the cab fare with the last of her cash. When the driver tipped his hat with the flash of an honest smile, she thought of warning him about icy mornings and following too closely behind delivery trucks. He only had two years left. Yet wouldn't he be all the more distraught if he saw his wife go first? What was eating at her insides wasn't treatable. Being alone was so much worse than dying.

She knocked again on Gerald's door and noticed the neatness of the yard. She tasted fire and truth and enemies who had become lovers. Everything was possible.

Gerald opened the front door and the screen too. Lily watched him from the corner of her eye.

"Lily?" he asked.

"Mm-hmm."

"You came back?"

"Just like you were hoping."

She held up the cookies she'd made for him, soft in the middle, burned around the edges. He practically fell over himself taking the plate and asked her inside. She did and he wasted no time begging for her forgiveness.

"I was so wrong," he began and said all the things she'd hoped. He'd taken her for granted. She meant everything. They needed to be together. He meant it, too. Every word.

When he wrapped her in his arms and kissed her deeply, she returned his affections. It went on and on. His hands roamed. With the gesture now less an avowal and more of a bedroom warm-up, she pushed him away.

"Thank you. This is how I always imagined it," she said. "When did you take him?"

He shook his head slowly. His smile hesitated, but rose again.

"That first night?" she asked. "Be honest."

"I don't know what you—"

"My god, Dice. If I could tell before, why wouldn't I be able to see it now?"

Gerald's body shifted uneasily. Within it, Dice struggled to size up Lily, and a nervous tension crossed the brow. "He was a waste," she said. "Until I saved him."

"You murdered him."

"Maybe. You don't seem that bothered."

"I envy him. He's with her now."

"That part of his being, yes. The rest," Dice motioned to her new frame, the sad paunch and pale arms, "is yours. I'm giving him to you."

"You're not what he was."

"Don't be naive. He wasn't loyal. Do you know how easy it was to bed him?" When Lily winced and looked away, Dice corrected, "Wait, I didn't mean—"

The shadows in the room shifted. The Child of Sheol crouched near, but Dice didn't notice, not even when the beast swallowed them both. All her years of experience and yet this profundity was invisible to her. It proved how special Lily was. She cupped Dice's cheeks in her hands.

"We're in the chapel."

Within this hallowed place, anything could happen. Souls could be joined.

"Yes," Dice sighed. "This is what you wanted, what I wanted. It's too wonderful not to be right. We'll be what each other needs and everything will be perfect. Call me with his name, if it makes it easier. Now he loves you."

She hugged Lily tight.

"I never realized how lonely you were," Lily said.

"I was. For a lifetime."

"I have something special for you."

"Oh?" Dice said breathily.

"From me it's done softly." Lily drew her mouth close. "Stay with me."

Her lips touched Dice's. Her mind followed. Within the shadows, in the bowels of Sheol, they embraced to a divine voice whispering cold words. Dice's eyes flew open, and she whimpered a plea which may have been gratitude. She was eclipsed.

Lily's old body crumpled to the floor.

It took hours for the dizziness to fade. Lily traced fingertips over her new profile and struggling hairline. She undressed and studied herself from every angle, poking and pinching and feeling curious new sensations. As the goddess had instructed, she'd taken him. His body wasn't much to look at, but she would call it home, for a while.

A warmth stirred deep within her, close to her bones. She tasted old memories, bits and pieces of lives gathered like a bird's nest. She held dozens of daughters and sons, every one of them hers. When they turned their first gaze to her face, she sobbed with relief.

And it didn't need to end here. She could go wherever she pleased. She could be a husband or a wife, a child or a mother. She had an eternity to sample humanity. No, not quite. Strange constellations drifted closer. Some things were eternal, but not all.

The van was parked in the alley behind the house. She backed it up to the garage and after a bit of maneuvering, shelved her old body. She turned her senses to the city.

Three more.

KEYS IN STRANGER DESERTS

Vrai Kaiser

IT TOOK THREE YEARS OF STUDY, endless summers of extracurricular padding, and a fleet of recommendations (though none, spiting popular rumor, were required to be sealed in blood—which didn't stop me from surreptitiously dribbling a few blots onto the postage stamps to cover my bases) to gain admittance to Miskatonic University, and the course of one afternoon for me to leave it. The end result had a lot to do with the suited figure sitting across from me, though it had started long before her.

"I hear you tried to steal the *Necronomicon*." She propped her chin on her hand, seemingly boneless with confidence as she draped across the leather armchair.

"Bullshit!" This was the fifth third degree I'd had in as many hours, and maybe my nerves were a little tender. I tried to reel back. "If that's what they told you they're liars. I had a senior student to make sure everything went back where it was supposed to. Real supervision and everything." At this she raised a skeptical eyebrow, but I was already tired of having that particular argument with the higher-ups. "Nothing would have left the collection."

"So, why the lock pick?" Her booted foot was twitching a *tap-tap-tap* on the Dean's ornate carpet. So gracious of him to lend us this room, symbolically declaring they were done with me even if the paperwork hadn't been signed.

"I got tired of jumping through their hoops."

My focus on a practical education drowned almost immediately in the thick atmosphere of Arkham. I was lulled by whispers at the orientation and stories traded by bonfire on the coast, sated by legends of stuffed tweed suits who'd gone mad and cars full of undergraduates who never returned from adventures to neighboring inlets. With all those distractions, it was almost a full year before I ran into my first roadblock.

Despite a mild dose of notoriety that emerged from its medical department, I imagine you know about the true crown jewel of Miskatonic: its library of rare books, dusty manuscripts spotted with blood and the spittle of the raving tenured, some rumored to be bound in the flesh of human skin. I immediately put in a request for an afternoon in the collection.

"I'm afraid that access to those volumes is limited to postgraduate study and guided mentorships." The desk clerk frowned over his typewriter, handing my application back. For a minute his eyes raked past the soft fuzz that remained of my natural hair, and I bristled instinctively.

"Isn't there some kind of exception? Do you need someone in there to make sure I won't rip any pages out? I don't mind. I just, I have to—" I found myself at a loss to explain the *why* of this driving urge. Sinking every hour I had into studying for a decent scholarship hadn't left me with a cultivated taste for campfire stories, and I had entered orientation fully intending to enter some field of practical, financially soluble work. But even now, just thinking about it, I was once again folded into a stranger's bunk at two in the morning with their voice washing over me.

"So finally, three days out on this rickety old boat, he sees it. Something beneath the water." And here the senior paused, reeling their audience in. *"It's a city. Even though the water can't be more than ten feet deep, he knows he could reach down for a mile and never grasp it. And he starts crying, like that's the end of his life right there if he can't reach out to one of those deep, mossy spires. And the lady on the wharf who had to pull him out, she says,*

'*Crazy bastard just fell in! Started sinkin' like a rock.*'

But she says it with this echo, like she's squintin' at something with her voice. When the paramedics found them she'd been doing resuscitation on the old man for almost thirty minutes, but nothing. He keeps breathing, but he won't wake up.

'*He just kept coughin' up water. Musta been a gallon,*' *she swears.*

They take him to the hospital and leave him there, holding down an old bed like a paperweight. They're waiting for something to happen. And one night the night nurse comes in, and he almost throws up. It stinks like a barrel of bloating fish in there, and the floor's covered in a long, slimy trail that starts at the window and stops at the bed. And the old man's eyes are finally open, staring at nothing. He's cold and stiff, like he's been dead for days, even though they checked on him that morning. And there's a grin on his face, bigger than what should fit on a human skull."

Looking back in the cold light of day, it was easy to start poking holes in the story. How did they know what the man had seen, if he'd been in a coma? How could some unearthly visitor enter from nowhere and leave a visible sign of its presence? Why the hell would it bother? But no matter how many skeptical needles I produced, none of them could deflate the awe that now sparked in my chest at the mere mention of the preternatural.

From the day of that first rejection I made the library my home. I made stubborn eye contact with the clerk every morning, taking a stack of books for study in what I'd nominally declared a Classics major. Like most curriculums at Miskatonic, it was all about planning one's course of study around the best access to your particular peculiarities. I would sit in view of the locked reading rooms, paging through books cross-referenced to any word in the card catalogue that might be even tenuously connected to what I was seeking.

That was the trouble, of course. I was digging after a feeling supposed by a dead man, with nothing to anchor it in the geography of academia. The librarians who'd acted as secondary parents in my childhood hadn't taught me how to accommodate for this many unknowns. Three weeks in I wasn't accomplishing anything but coming in with my cold, habitual "*Terry*" to the front desk and then wasting three hours learning about the horrible minutiae of crustacean exoskeletons, making a show of how much I deserved to be there, and not absorbing a damn thing.

When I wasn't at the library, I was concocting reasons for why my professors absolutely needed to help me plan an extracurricular study course—you had to say it that way, since the creation of a syllabus lent it a feeling of gravitas. Every one of them came back with the same response.

"Your work is exceptional, Ms. Devereux, but I'm afraid your suggested topics require a firmer grasp of context. Maybe in a few years..."

Or some variation thereof. It was just after sophomore midterms, and I had chosen the furthest table still technically in view of the coveted private library. It was a good spot for holding back a frustrated cry, allowing a slip up every so often that prickled the seams of my eyelids. That was when Darlene found me.

She was a senior, wearing a wool skirt and sweater so out of date she must've asked H.G. Wells to help her shop. Her hair was up in bobby pins, and there was a real sophisticated air about her when she wanted it. Boys hung around her at an appropriate distance, and her grades were good-not-great in every class. The perfect WASP veneer. The armchair set loved it.

"You look downright lovesick." She greeted me, spinning a chair under her hand before noticing a small study group out of the corner of her eye and redirecting herself to sit, primly, on the edge of the seat.

"What's it to you?" I grumbled, too tired to snap.

She leaned in, laying a gentle pat on my arm. Her grin was pointed. "Two grand in a betting pool. I laid odds on December 18th. Makes it a nice Christmas gift for you, see? And me."

"Came over here just to gloat?"

Her eyes widened, genuine, for almost a second. Then the nonchalance settled back in. "Why bother? You're going through hell as it is. I say why not make it work for both of us."

On the one hand, I was shooting myself in the foot. On the other, I was tired of seeing moldering book covers in my dreams and fighting the urge to trip Terry down the stairs. And Darlene's reputation was sterling.

"... I'm listening."

✳

The stranger frowned, one gloved hand paging through a pocketbook. "Darlene..."

"That's not her name, so don't bother." What did this woman take me for? "Just bringing this down on me is enough."

"My apologies. Go on." I could feel the woman's eyes on me from behind her tinted glasses, but her hand kept paging at that little book.

"So, that night..."

Once you've spent a year of your life someplace, the ins and the outs start sinking into you. It was surprisingly easy to be where the night watch wasn't, and after an hour there wasn't a whisper of human life outside my own mystified footsteps. Mission or not, I was struck still by the transformation the building had undergone. Pale light shrouded the stacks from the high windows of the main hall, and without the constant whisper of moving bodies there was a low, vibrating hum that hung just below conscious thought and prickled at the base of my spine. I put out my hand, certain that if I grasped the corner of the scene before me it would peel away, revealing some second truth that would gnaw at the marrow of my bones and twist tendrils around my brain while it whispered secrets long forgotten. I reached—

"Hey!" It was the lowest summons, but it shattered me. My door retreated, and I turned to find my probable guide.

"Will you meet me there?"

"What're you, crazy?" Darlene had scoffed. *"I'll send somebody, don't worry. Strictly up and up."*

He was small and round, bundled in a heavy coat and a hat out of something noir. I smiled at him, face stricken to rictus by nerves, and he motioned me over toward the coveted door.

It felt almost like defilement, watching him crouch before the shiny new lock set in the warped wood. I almost told him to stop, but my voice was stoppered by the image of the library, the air itself transforming into a door begging to be opened. *How dare they?* The image asked me. *How dare they set a safeguard on knowledge?*

A tumbler clicked, and my guide motioned me into the room ahead of him. It was smaller than I'd imagined it from the outside, its four squat bookshelves crushed by their own confinement. And there, guarded behind a glass case, was my prize. I knew it instinctively, guided by rumors and something deeper, and the prickle in my spine returned. I motioned the other student over to the glass case. I'd brought latex gloves and face masks and insisted that he put them on before so much as touching the case's lock. I followed suit with trembling hands, and no sooner had I protected the book from my touch than it was in my hands. It sang hello, and I smiled as I sat down to open its pages.

And then it was morning, and Terry was staring down at my book and I with a wall of security at his back.

"That's it?" The woman sat up, her sudden stiffness highlighted all the more by her prior nonchalance. "That's the good part?"

I shrugged. The Dean hadn't believed me either, though there had been a certain solemn recognition in the head librarian's face when I described the blank space in my memory. "It's how it is. Take it or leave it."

"So you don't remember anything," she pressed. Her free hand began to drum on the arm rest.

"What's it to you?"

The question hung on a precipice, and then she had swung her weight so that both feet rested on the ground, her gaze intent on me. "Nichelle—"

"Dev." My mother had watched *Star Trek* on public broadcast with stars in her eyes, and I'd never felt up to the name of a woman who'd inspired other children to run for the stars.

"Andre," she replied, sticking out the introductory hand she'd forgotten about when she'd marched in over an hour ago. I let it curl up and die in the air, until it retreated into removing those dark glasses. Her eyes were green.

"Listen," she said. "We're in the same boat, you and I. I'm crazy to learn about this stuff, but the snobs up here look at me and see a two-bit nobody not even worth thumbing their nose at."

In spite of myself, I bit. "What *stuff*?"

"Doors to other worlds, monsters in the hills. Shimmering cities you can't touch no matter how close you get to 'em. Real pulp novel stuff.

Only it isn't, is it?" There was suddenly precious little air between us. "It's in that book of yours."

There hadn't been much time between coming to and being frogmarched down to my current imprisonment to savor the moment. Even now I wasn't certain I could put it into words. Like being stretched thin with knowing, able to see a great certainty but not quite able to break through. My body had ached, was still throbbing, but my mind was a cavern of jagged knives.

"I remember a few things," I couched.

At that she smiled, leaning back into a repose of victory. "Then I have a few things I've remembered to ask you."

While Miskatonic campus was in possession of several dingy but functional phone booths, I didn't bother to phone my parents when I was escorted out. It would have required explaining how I had ended up first in the passenger seat of a late-model Bentley that probably cost more than a year's tuition, seated next to a probable con artist twice my age and agreeing to accompany her to an unknown destination after narrowly escaping arrest for breaking and entering. My tongue shriveled at the mere thought of where to begin. My mother had wanted the stars for me, after all. And deeper than that, something had been singing to me since the night before, urging me forward.

"The way I see it," Andre was saying as we bumped down a poorly maintained highway, "it's no good for those ivory tower types to keep all the good news to themselves." She pointed vaguely in a direction I took to be south. "The government's already got that locked up with that weather balloon crap."

"You think they've found something in the crash?" The idea of keeping not just a wreck but actual living beings hidden from the public eye seemed sinister in a way I hadn't, before now, imagined.

"C'mon, kid, I thought you were smart. Don't go disappointing me now." She stubbed her cigarette and tossed it out the window. "You're old enough to remember Tricky Dick, and you think they can't hide a couple alien bodies out in the middle of the desert?"

Invaders from beyond the stars sleeping in the earth. I shivered. "Is that what you wanted me for?" If so, she was going to be disappointed.

The creatures in Miskatonic's poorly collected firsthand accounts weren't little grey men looking to show us strange galaxies. They were unspeakable shapes and colors with no names, seething through the backwoods unlike any Universal monster.

"Hold your horses. For someone who staked a place out for a year, you're awful impatient." And then we drove in silence for three hours— her smirking in the light of oncoming cars, me determined to hold my pride.

We stopped for the night at a motel and made camp at the small table, which was no longer than my forearm. I nursed a cup of coffee, watching her watch me.

"Let's start easy." She lit another cigarette, using the glowing end like a pointer in the dim light. "Where do we have to go? There's some pilgrimage, yeah? See the big tentacled beastie where he sleeps?"

"It depends on what you're looking for," I said. "There are accounts at least a century back around Massachusetts and New England of strange occurrences, but I think that's just what Miskatonic bothered to collect."

"Real saturated, I'll give it that," Andre mumbled.

"But the original translation of the *Necronomicon* was in Arabic. A door in the middle of the desert..." I trailed off, frozen by thoughts racing under my conscious mind.

That caught her attention. "Could be anywhere, then. That's good. Like the, uh...Shangri-La of your soul, that type of thing."

I didn't respond, but it didn't seem to matter much. She kept on a low prattle of ideas spoken to a stubby tape recorder, and I attempted to detach my eyes enough to hold onto the shadows that kept hiding behind my retinas.

The revelation that we needn't stay bound to the orbit of Massachusetts turned a meandering journey into a hellbent one. We traded the uneven highway for the interstate, roaring past whole states only to slow to a sputter and hit every town along a single rural stretch. At these spots Andre would disappear into a coffee house or a gas station and appraise the situation. If she sat down it would be an hour or more, and I'd follow her in, pluck some reading material from the nearest shelf and make do.

Other times she'd eye the farmers having coffee or slouching teenagers dreaming of better days and find them lacking, and off we would go.

At first, I tried listening in on them. Andre had a different voice for every group. She'd take off her sharp-cut suit jacket and slip into a worn button up before sauntering over to a scuffed table. "Mind if I sit?" She'd ask, casual but deferring, to the worn out drivers in wide brim caps. Into the third cup or so, she'd start talking, about seeing the stars on the road at night and the universe. About how she'd been a Christian woman, but it was hell trying to find peace constantly shuttling between one life and the next. Then, if they started nodding (and if they were sleepy enough to take it all in, placid), she'd drop a few things about "somethin' beyond what we can see, right at our fingertips."

If her audience had leather jackets she'd put on something jittering in her stance, a look like hell was chasing after her. She'd talk about some all-consuming black. "The doors in the desert," I heard her lace in, and part of me prickled with a sense of betrayal. But it didn't mean much in eighty degree heat in the middle of nowhere, not with empty pockets and an emptier stomach. "Doesn't this kind of racket usually have a pamphlet?" I asked after a week, snatching the greasy offered bag from her fingertips.

"That's amateur hour," she replied, watching the traffic pass over another cup of coffee. "You gotta know how to let a legend simmer. Rumors have to seem natural when they spread. The rich thrill seeker type loves to feel like they're getting in on something real edgy, and nobody with actual brain cells will bother to tell them otherwise. It's all big picture stuff, kid. Whole big world outside those books of yours."

It became a routine. After a day of talking we'd stop at another motel with Andre's seemingly bottomless wallet, and she would sit me down and ply me for what I remembered. In my sleep it was bursts of color on my tongue, but in the lamplight it all went dry.

"Goddammit, what'd I bring you for?" she swore one night, keyed up on a day of bad bites.

"Guessing you mistook me for one of the books they wouldn't let you have." The further we got from the coast the more my dreams seemed to retreat. I was starting to wonder if I'd been wrong, and the magic really was laced in that heavy northeastern fog.

"I'm paying for an expert, not a charity case."

I watched her walk out into the parking lot and slam the door behind her, and it was only when I heard the Bentley's engine that a spark of panic lit in me. What the hell was I supposed to do in Wisconsin? Did they even have trains here? Did buses stop? I wanted to run after her into the night, so I forced myself to kick off my shoes and flip the TV on. The static became a comfortable background to my thoughts, and I counted my breaths. Not sure how long I'd be alone, I tried to reach back to that night at the library.

The pages were warm under my fingers, and when I touched them I was certain I had done so a hundred times, and a thousand times before that. Each successive seeker of knowledge grasped my hand and helped to turn over the heavy blocks of text. Their hollow eyes could no longer see it, but still they took up their places as signposts to the next generation.

If I wanted, I could bring them back. We could hold court in the fields, and stare beyond the holes to the shambling truths beyond. I looked back to the page—

A wad of plastic *thunked* against my forehead. The hotel room washed back over me, dingy and stale. Grey light streamed in from the window. I blinked down at the foreign object: a handful of round blue pills in a plastic bag. Oxycodone.

"Make that last." Audrey was kicking the door shut. "Took me a day and a half to get that much."

As she said it, I realized that my legs were riddled with pins, my lower back in agony. I had gone drifting on Sunday night, and the morning weather report now said Tuesday. I tried to move, gritting my teeth at every agonizing inch. "Is that—"

"Yeah, and it wasn't cheap, either. Hide it somewhere and let's get going. I wanna make it to spitting distance of Kansas before it gets dark."

I balled up the bag and chucked it, narrowly missing her head. "Are you trying to get me shot?"

"It's fine. I know how to keep the cops off us. Quit worryin', already."

"No, no way. I'm done." I stumbled toward the door, still feeling numb. "I don't know what the hell I'm doing here, anyway. And you—"

"Hey! Hey, hey, whoa whoa whoa. Let's stay calm here." She caught my arm as I reached for the door, which turned half into a cradling hold as my knees mutinied. "I'm just trying to help, here."

"By getting me locked up? Do you know the time I'd get for just looking at that stuff?"

"No, look, it's not that bad. They're prescription, alright? They're mine. Nobody's gonna look twice at it if I keep it." She bent down to retrieve the bag, keeping eye contact like I was some spooked gazelle. "Just thought it might help you remember some stuff. I heard it around that you academic types sometimes need help 'communing with the other side.'"

Now that my legs were regaining feeling, it was easy to notice the separate ache that had started when I returned from my uncompleted memory. The burn of not knowing was physical, like staring wide-eyed into an over chlorinated swimming pool. I stared at the pills, at the con who'd spirited me away.

"You'd better tell me exactly what you need all this information for."

She grinned. With the smudge on her lipstick, it looked feral.

"Deal."

Andre had designs on a castle. "The kind of place people'll come to from all over, seeking that truth. We put 'em up—for a few dimes— offer to guide them to squishy extraterrestrial enlightenment, ba*bam*. Everybody's happy."

I sank down into the now familiar leather, pondering my life choices. "You want to start a cult?"

"It's only a cult if what you're selling is crap." She glanced at me from the corner of her eye. "So, is it a cult?"

I started opening the door toward incoming traffic, and she relented, swerving to avoid the shriek of oncoming horns. The rest of the drive was quiet.

That night, on the border of Utah, I swallowed the first of the pills. Feeling nothing, I took advantage of my audience. "Where do you expect to find a castle, anyway?"

"Nevada is a place of wonders, my young friend." Andre was in a sparkling mood, an open bottle of gin in one hand so that she could "keep me company." She took a swig, not so much as flinching.

"You wouldn't believe what they built out there before the economy went to shit."

"Which time?"

"I'm very impressed, professor. Point is, we find one to repurpose. Problems solved."

I yawned. "I thought I was here in a strictly advisory capacity."

"You? Hey, none of this happens without you. Partner-like, Dev-dev-i-to. Fifty-fifty." She smacked me hard on the back. The ringing aftermath of it pried into my ears, making them into fathomless canyons. I skated across them to the other side, combing particles of thought through my fingers.

Five fathoms deep and down further still, I shed a toll of tars for my lost cousin, dead and sleeping in the ditch. He expanded to greatness I could not contain, and yet I would travel further than he ever would again. Beneath me the ground became sulfuric snaps of flesh consuming itself, full of violet light that chilled me and sent aching thrums through my head. Senses blurred together and lost meaning, scrambling signals from one receptor to another. And I wept again, because this was not my circle of scholars. I had opened a door down a new path meant for other travelers, and now the knob was slipping from my grip. I'd wander here, and find –

"—up!"

A cold shock doused me, banishing the image. Andre was kneeling over me, a telltale line creasing the center of her brow. Her breath smelled of gin-mint and menthol, and the overwhelming stimulus of it nearly sent my stomach into rebellion. When I could sit up she wrapped a towel around my shoulders and handed me a pencil, and repeated the movement until my fingers stopped shaking enough to grasp it.

"Write," she said, and I did. I stared off into the middle distance while I worked, and refused to look at it after. That was a stranger's epiphany, and I had no right to it.

She whistled low as she read the slanted scribblings and tucked them into her purse, plucking the pills from the bedside table as well. "Save that good stuff for when we get there."

For there did seem to be a *where* now, pinpointed at some point during my long and terrifying vacation. The Hard Luck Mine had been abandoned not long into the century, when the wars had struck and maddening sights had begun crawling the coast.

"Damn near perfect, isn't it?" Andre crowed, leaning out the window in defiance of the beating desert sun as we pulled up to the site. Barely into the New Year and it felt like summer. "Might even keep the name." We left the Bentley ticking over in the dust. She kicked rocks out of her way as she walked, leaving me to weave a trail behind her. "Eh, scratch that. Doesn't quite have a pretentious enough air."

"Mmm." If I blinked for too long the landscape turned into gibbets of meat, and an entire box of Andre's mints hadn't been able to purge the rotten taste from the corners of my mouth.

Andre was leaning over the massive hole that marked the mine's main entrance. "How many people you figure died down there?" She lobbed a rock in, and was still waiting for the bounce by the time I made it to the lip of the entrance. The shadow within was melting upward toward her, trying to take her in its arms and peel her into fragments, but by the time I opened my mouth to say something—

"Come on, inside. I've got a dream to market, my prophet's not dying of dehydration. That's a weak story to sell."

I couldn't stomach another pill, I insisted. This was the fifth day of the argument. "They're not for me," I insisted, pushing them back into Andre's hand with as firm a grip as I could still muster. Miskatonic seemed an eon away, not a few weeks. I was henpecked by my dreams, flailing for something that swam from me when I moved only to drag me with it, connected by a spear hooked under my ribs. If I lay still, I knew it would pull me up into the stars, and before the cold took me there would be some measure of peace.

"That's nice poetry, but it's a little death cult for this kind of venture. We want the sort with extra money to spend and too much to drink, alright? Rich eccentrics who wanna part with their money, not their lives."

I stared, puzzled. Then embarrassed, and not sure if it was at my mouth for speaking my thoughts without permission or my mind for becoming so dull and sluggish. I oozed through the days, listening to Andre whip her project into a formidable shape and nodding when the moment felt appropriate. At night I wandered outside, thinking about spaces between spaces and looking for where I might have left myself. Who was I?

The well, I answered myself. Unable to glean more than that, I picked a comfortable rock in sight of the hole and sat down to wait. What I was waiting for refused to so much as hint at itself.

When night fell I was vaguely aware of Andre shepherding me inside the tower she'd repurposed as a base of sorts, her hands flinching every time I backed away from something in the corner of my eye. She all but tucked me into bed, tapping one finger against her leg as she stared down at me.

"Take the week off, huh?" she said at last. "Don't want you shambling in like some zombie when the customers get here."

When she had gone I reached for the small collection of paperbacks next to the bed. The words got up and walked, leading my eyes to strange shapes on the horizon and seismic shifts beneath my feet. There was something wonderful here, and terrible.

I snorted, wracked with a fit of laughter that wouldn't stop until my throat, dry and overworked, seized and turned to coughing. Andre's thrill seekers would find enlightenment after all, deeper than they'd ever prepared for.

Stumbling over to tell her the good news, I found the door locked.

An hour of shouting and beating against the wall left me with bruised fists and no response. I kept my eyes open as long as I could out of some warped spite, sinking down onto the inflatable mattress with my eyes locked on the door. The first lines of the hell I was going to give her rolled thick over my tongue, and my head filled with curses in dead languages half remembered.

"Stay focused," I repeated to myself, watching the walls slide and liquidate before snapping back to mundanity. Night passed overhead as a series of distant novas, their light as dead and indifferent as the voices now pressing into the back of my skull. Stars were beyond me. But their kin was waiting, reflecting my own impatience back to me.

I got up and walked.

If the discordant, hypnotic trip I'd taken before had been a broken mirror, then this was the glass made whole. Every step I took echoed with another foot that had fallen before, creating a roaring echo until I was weighted with centuries. And even still, I saw myself small. The crash of my feet was nothing, swallowed up by the hum of blackness. I might as well have not been there.

Then there's no reason to tell me I can't see whatever I want. A speck could float through any keyhole, observe any event without notice. Every book of knowledge lay discarded at my feet, open and unguarded. In the roar of the dark it was outdated and meaningless even before it was written, the afterimage of reality grasped only dimly. And yet, with it I could craft a universe.

Something stirred to my left—the door was open now, pulsing faintly. I nodded to it, picking up pages to scatter behind me as I walked. There was going unnoticed, and then there was carelessness.

I walked down winding stairs that descended to the core of the earth before spitting me out in the parking lot, where I could see Andre talking to a small gaggle of onlookers. Some had shoulders heavy with the weight of survival (and one, in a long duster, was a bright star in itself); others, in polo shirts and khakis, were so faded that I could barely see their outlines. But Andre...

My breath caught. The well was still reaching up to her, setting teeth at her ankles and eyes on her wrists, and now I could see why. Her torso was hollowed with caverns of impossible, ghastly liquid. It trickled down her sides and left grey, shriveled patches where it touched the earth. Her eyes were great globes filled with the screaming of the shambling Old Ones past, hungry and trapped by their inability to be recognized. The closer I looked, the more I saw. Every fingernail was a sliver of madness. Each blood vessel was a highway to greater understanding.

"I found them..." I breathed. Dead, not sleeping, waiting in our bones to be charmed out. The group of shadows turned to look at me, drawing themselves up tall and brittle.

"Andre. I figured out what you need to tell them." My stride shed its faltering. One, two, three, and we stood face to face. She burbled a response, black tar oozing from the corners of her mouth. Her hands shot out like claws, trying to take the information I no doubt held but couldn't see. The journey was different for everyone, after all. I put my hand out to show her, like I was turning the pages of the book, and grasped one of the hollows in her chest.

The tumblers clicked into place, and the door came open. The color soaked into the earth, burning it into polished glass, and in it I saw the tools to understanding. The orbs shattered, and I heard the screams of old eons returning to their owners. For a moment a great eye turned to me, and I saw myself through its gaze, which was also the whole world. I wept, knowing what I had to do then. I left.

The trembling limits of my frame solidified, stilled. The roar of the universe dimmed, receding into the pit behind me, and the faces before me donned their earthly masks. They looked, most understandably, confused.

At the back of the silent, gape-mouthed group was the duster-clad figure I had seen on the other side. Their long, dark hair fell over their eyes, but they didn't retreat as I approached and took their hand. It felt sticky in mine.

"Don't worry," I said. "It's different for everyone. We just have to find your door."

It was just the two of us now, and the sound of tires screeching on some other, unimportant plane. I let go of the stranger's hand, bending to pick up Andre's notepad as I made my way back inside. There would need to be a new book.

ἱερὸς γάμος
Hieros Gamos

Gord Sellar

THE MYSTIC CENTER OF THAT long-lost cult in Greece, ancient Eleusis, has been scratched away, a palimpsest overwritten by the steel and bricks and pavements of 1961. The commensurate stink of paint and concrete factories, and other industrial horrors, wafts over from the nearby town of Eleusinia. An endless cacophony of honking cars is faintly audible, too, even so far outside Athens—amid hills, even over the endless rasping waves of cicada-songs spewing from the grubby, misshapen trees perched here and there—and Dr. Shankar Bandyopadhyay briefly longs for the quiet of home. But home is distant now, he reminds himself, and if his suspicions are correct, then he will never truly go home again.

Such a long journey it has been, through hostile cities, rough towns, and stifling villages; the decades have been long, the miles countless. From colonial Calcutta, via London, Washington, and finally Venice and Athens, he has come to Eleusinia, and guided only by snippets in poems, by hints of a secret history he himself glimpsed in the lines of a madman's poetry. Such a long journey alone, and so very little more to go before his convictions are either vindicated or crushed.

Now seems as good a moment as any for a moment of rest, so he takes a seat on a large, flat-headed stone nearby. He recalls some lines from the draft of an old lunatic's abandoned poem: "Ghosts move about me / patched with histories..." Bandyopadhyay squints, as if expecting to behold spectres all about him now; imagining some hidden, ancient arena and himself seated on the steps, a spectator to the unfolding of the cumulative blood and horror of all ages past. He aches for a vision of the ancient cultists: devotees drinking the sacred, intoxicating *kykeon* of barley and pennyroyal, and pausing at the entrance of the great hall to chant their sacred phrase before entering.

At the center of that great imagined hall, a glimmering palace stands, open only to the Hierophants of the highest order. Within its walls, the greatest of Mysteries occurs: descent into the underworld, and the *hieros gamos*—that mystical marriage rite at the heart of the Eleusinian Mystery cult, said to unlock godlike powers and bathe the mind in the shimmering eternal light of divine consciousness. The heart of light, shining within the shadowy chambers of that palace of the center of Demeter's Temple.

Yet Bandyopadhyay glimpses none of these things, not even the shadow of Alaric the Visigoth, the temple's final destroyer, who left this place in ruins. There is nothing more mystical than the honking of distant cars, the stink of the nearby factories, the sun sinking brilliant and fiery toward the smog-clouded horizon. He coughs slightly, takes a sip of water from a flask, and then he rises to his feet.

A voice, speaking in Greek, shatters his solitude.

Bandyopadhyay spins, half-expecting an ancient apparition summoned by his yearnings—a young Emperor Julian, perhaps, reenacting the fateful night of his initiation?—but it is only a sweaty, balding Greek man, with a clipboard and a buttoned-down white shirt stretched across his pot-belly and stained with sweat at the armpits.

"Pardon me?" Bandyopadhyay says.

"Why are you here?" the Greek man asks him. Speaking English, his voice is much higher-pitched, more terrier than bullmastiff.

"I am a scholar..." Bandyopadhyay says. "I have spent years researching the Eleusinian mysteries, and simply wanted to see..." Though he is not a talented liar, he judges his performance adequate.

"You should not be here. Not allowed," says the grim-faced Greek, wielding his clipboard like some sort of administrative weapon that could bureaucratize a person away, perhaps clean out of existence.

Bandyopadhyay lets his shoulders slump. Arriving as a dark-skinned foreigner in London, no less, at a time when India had still been a part of the Empire, he'd already known to switch personae as needed. He'd bluffed his way into barred, secret libraries this way, had convinced paranoiacs to spill their arcana to him, and had even infiltrated supposedly impenetrable conspiracies with nothing more than the right muttered words and a slight contortion of his facial muscles.

"...this site...still excavating. You mustn't disturb..."

The Indian nods, thinking briefly of Demeter, of Lakshmi and Saranyu; of Persephone clawing her way up out of the black soil, her chin stained with a fine trail of pomegranate juice. He circles a word in his mind, a secret word he does not allow himself to think directly, allowing it only to drift blurrily at the edge of his consciousness, unreadable and unrecognizable. The word sets like a fog-muddled sun into the underworld of his mind. It is unwise to be too blunt in one's theurgy, after all, he reminds himself; he'd learned that years before, during a misadventure in Singapore.

The Greek's attitude softens suddenly, and Bandyopadhyay must fight not to grin in triumph.

"Well, it would be a shame...if you came all this way for nothing." The archaeologist glances around quickly, and then cocks his head to one side. "Have you found the *Telesterion*?"

Bandyopadhyay casts the Greek a funny look: "Telesterion" is the name of the grand hall, that place he had tried to imagine earlier. "Was it not here?"

It is the Greek's turn to laugh, and he shakes his head. "Here? Just toilets and rocks. Come on," and then he leads Bandyopadhyay a short distance away. He must be an archaeologist, Bandyopadhyay realizes.

Perhaps it is the gorgeous sunset, which has turned most of the sky fiery; or perhaps the way the cicadas suddenly fall silent as the light dims. Or just his imagination, perhaps? Something sets to standing on end the hairs on the back of the Indian's neck, along with those on his arms and on his legs in their loose-fitting suit pants. And the Greek man stops, too, turning to face Bandyopadhyay.

"What do you study?" the Greek archaeologist asks.

"Ah...a mixture of things, sir," Bandyopadhyay replies. Too many questions would mean trouble. Nothing good could come of discussing Mead and Pound, mentioning Péladan and Blavatsky and the Hidden Vedas, explaining the heretic Albigensian troubadours and the Manicheans of Xinjiang—that whole secret history of the world, the celestial tradition that had, after all, been occulted for a reason. He smiles as he meets the Greek's eye. "Literature..." he says, so softly the word might be lost among the crepuscular rasping of the cicadas. "...mythology..."

"Well, then Greece is right place for you!" the man declares, chuckling as if he's being disingenuous, and looks up into the darkening sky. "Here," he says, pointing to a patch of ground some distance ahead of them. Bandyopadhyay squints, but there is too little light to see where or what the man is indicating.

"Don't worry, I'll bring you," the archaeologist says with a reluctant smile, and he produces a small torch from a pocket of his trousers. Flicking the switch, he floods the ground up ahead with a stark, whitish light. All around, enormous shadows sway about the light's edges, like great black creatures wandering the late dusk and eager to avoid being seared by it.

They walk together a little, until suddenly the archaeologist stops again.

"Here, they spoke phrase, before entering the *Telesterion*." Bandyopadhyay knows the phrase, or rather its equivalent in English; his ancient Greek is rather poor, truth be told. But the archaeologist intones a series of alien syllables slowly, gazing at the Indian as does so. "You say also," he urges, and repeats himself, pausing often to allow Bandyopadhyay carefully to twist his lips and tongue around the unfamiliar sounds. After the last syllable, the Indian scholar finds himself slightly woozy.

But he takes a deep breath, seeking both reassurance and joy in his triumph: he is finally here, at the temple of Demeter, after all these years of study, after all the exhausting journeys and disappointments. The lies of the yogis of his youth, and the sad pointlessness of the cell where Mani, the Manicheans' prophet, died in the ancient Sassanid Empire's capital; the Church of St. Hilaire in Poitiers, and the barren peak of

Montségur; in the Tempio di Malatesta in Rimini, Italy, beside the remains of Gemisthus Plethon, and the place where it was said Kung had died...all those false leads, those lies...somehow, they have led him here, prepared him for this night.

"They drank *kykeon* here, at the threshold, as well, did they not?" he asks the Greek, who nods.

"After fasting...not eating," the Greek says, nodding.

"Well, I have fasted," Bandyopadhyay blurts out, before adding with a smile, "In a manner of speaking." He fetches a flask from his shoulder bag. After unscrewing the top and drinking a mouthful, he holds it out: "Will you have some?"

The Greek laughs, and nods. "Why not?" He takes a deep draught from it, perhaps expecting whiskey. When he tastes it—sweet malted barley, and the minty bitterness of the pennyroyal infusion—his eyes widen. Bandyopadhyay smiles: the man *recognizes* the toxic herb's flavor, clearly, and yet he drinks.

This is a man who has tasted *kykeon* before.

The Greek step backs, regarding Bandyopadhyay with something like distrust, and says, "We find no relics here. They were burned, maybe, or carried off. Nobody knows—it was written nowhere—what they were..."

"But it is probable," Bandyopadhyay says, smiling, "...that they would have included a sheaf of grain, some pomegranate seeds, a scythe, and a furrow in the ground. The Hierophant would have plunged into that furrow, to light the fire that burned through the holy night."

The archaeologist regards Bandyopadhyay for a moment with what looks like amusement before turning his back to the Indian scholar. "You should be careful. Too much of that—even a little too much— can kill you," he says, and while Bandyopadhyay knows he means the pennyroyal, he is also certain that is not all the man means.

"Come," the Greek says, and he sets out across the grounds of what was the great hall. They are, Bandyopadhyay knows, heading toward what doubtless was—<u>aeons</u> ago—the site of the great inner palace: the great *Anaktoron* into which only the great Hierophant of the Mysteries of Eleusis could enter.

And in the deepening gloom, following this man to the ruins of the greatest secret in history, Bandyopadhyay finds himself laughing too, aloud, a growling laugh surfacing from deep within him. The apparition of so many crowded faces flash before his eyes—the jail-mad old poet Ezra Pound in the asylum in Washington a few years before, ranting; and the hard-eyed old ex-banker, T.S. Eliot, retired in London and clinging to his crucifix even now, after all he had seen; the decrepit, credulous old theosophists creeping about among the ruins of lost Kensington, haunting their occult bookshops and babbling mingled half-truths about the fate of Blavatsky's Seven Worlds, that mad old woman, that wondrous old charlatan seventy years in the ground already. All these fools, black petals clinging to a dead, fallen bough. The disdain of poets, occultists, and Calcutta sadhus had burdened him throughout his quest, all these long years full of dark, strange nights. But now, finally, he whom they had mocked, Bandyopadhyay, stands at the threshold of the mother of all secrets.

As his laughter calms, Bandyopadhyay discovers that silence has filled the night: no more cars honking, only stillness. The stink of the factories has been vanquished by an otherworldly aroma, like tilled earth and blossoms and honey and something at once metallic, sugary, and fungal. The lights of the city are not distant, but far enough that the site is dark, and Bandyopadhyay can imagine the ancient initiates of Eleusis gazing up into a sky almost the same as he sees above—*almost*, but for the subtle shifting of the stars. Here, a fire would have burned, the Hierophant before it, or beside it—or some had hinted, *within* it.

As a wave of dizziness washes over Bandyopadhyay's mind, he recognizes the greater tidal shift that has been working upon the shore of his consciousness. *The kykeon.* Overhead, without fanfare or fuss, the stars begin to flicker and gutter, going out one by one. As the sky darkens, faint curtains of stars shimmer in the distance, vanishing next—swallowed by ravenous oblivion—in a slow, arcing sweep of light-silence, leaving a few small pinpricks of throbbing light, low in the sky; and beyond them, faintly glittering, other tiny pinpricks of light tinged with colors nameless and unseen to human eyes; the freakish light deepens to fill the whole sky.

"You see them?" asks the Greek, and without looking Bandyopadhyay knows that the man is seeing the same thing as he is, though with a calmness that suggests he has seen it before. Bandyopadhyay does not answer, but follows the shapes that coalesce in the blinding light, moving, shifting...descending toward the Earth.

The alien colors of the deepest regions of space turn and begin to throb, now, as pinpricks of that shimmering color from other worlds open across the sky. It is as if alien light were seeping through the pores of the universe itself, to stain the sky with their impossible colors. These pinpoints congeal above, taking on semi-physical forms both senseless and baffling, light spun into unthinkable constellations of matter, and they begin to drift in the air like gods, like pollen, almost-azure and not-rose and the darkness hidden in bright wine all melded together into unnameable hues. From the invisible follicles of the sky, the light spills forth, pouring down into the Earth all around Bandyopadhyay and the Greek... *cultist*, Bandyopadhyay dimly realizes.

For his part, Bandyopadhyay neither moves nor even tears his gaze from the leaking, iridescent sky above. The ground beneath their feet begins to tremble. A noise like nothing Bandyopadhyay has ever heard issues forth from the ground—a million voices crying out, the Sirens heard at sea by Odysseus, invisible chimeric mouths crammed full of slick and gleamingly brilliant tongues calling to him. A groan deep in the Earth echoes through his bones, sets his legs quivering, and suddenly, the sky bursts, light exploding out into the darkness between the disappeared stars, all the stars not yet born, all the stars that have died and left their radiant wreckage spattered across the heavens.

Only when the lights above turn blinding, and the pain forces him to avert his gaze, does Bandyopadhyay look to the ground. He finds it is as bright nearly as daylight, though swept by frightening, unnameable colors. Nearby, where the Greek had told him the *Anaktoron* had stood, a wide, raw furrow has opened itself in the earth, a mouth yawning wide in the not-darkness, sloping down into a pit brimming with light, with incredible screaming music, with such raw energy that he almost cannot resist its call.

The Greek's mouth is still moving, inaudible in the cacophony, muttering his incantations in some inhuman tongue that yanks the man's lips into impossible configurations. Bandyopadhyay is certain the man has been praying all the while. Praying, or chanting; perhaps some sort of theurgical binding? Immobile, the Indian scholar stares in dread as the cultist finishes his incantation and, smiling cruelly, moves toward him.

Bandyopadhyay steps backward, away from the Greek, but his assailant is quicker, and seizes him with both his hands—one at the throat, the other at the shoulder—and forces him backward, toward the pit.

Silently, with a short, sharp jolt, the Greek shoves him, sending him tumbling down.

In the now-dark pit, Bandyopadhyay feels as if the spell has faded somewhat. He is unable to flee, but he knows that flight would be madness anyway. Here awaits the *palingenetic* ritual of his transformative rebirth—his own Ovidian metamorphosis; here in the pit, buried in the sweet dark cthonic womb of Eleusis, lies the most esoteric coital magic of the ancients, the sacred marriage called *hieros gamos*. This is the hidden divine secret he has sought, buried at the heart of every occult tradition. Here, Parvati and Laksmi and Demeter and Aphrodite lie bare-fleshed, awaiting his embrace, waiting to make him a god. Here writhes the agent of his own long-sought transmogrification.

And nearby, something stirs in the darkness, and Bandyopadhyay stiffens, bending his head down. Man should be humble before gods, he knows, and yet he fights to maintain a little dignity, a little gravity.

Suddenly, the interior of the pit is scalded with searing light, as intense as the roiling luminosity of the transformed sky was above, outside. Bandyopadhyay flinches, but painful as the light is, it beckons him toward it. He begins to whisper too, as the Greek did above ground: Kali, Lakshmi, Demeter, Persephone, Koré, Guan Yin, Mary—the name of every female divinity he can recall. He speaks them not for the benefit of the presence in the pit, but rather only as a mantra for himself, to prevent his own mind from shattering under the pressure of what must be the *epopteia*—the holy vision of the celebrant of the Mysteries. He is drawn toward the strange, shifting wall of bright, shivering flesh, smooth as the flesh of a child, but puckered by a million mouths singing, smooth lips parting and grasping. It makes him think of the horror of smallpox turned somehow gorgeous. He stumbles toward it, drawn closer, and in an instant, the light flares, and all the feeble human raiments he has worn into this place—his sweat-soaked cotton shirt, his wrinkled khaki pants, his stinking leather shoes—are burnt away in a flash, leaving him like a child before its mother, like a beast in the wilderness: a man naked of the world, trembling before the divine.

The voices of the mouths—the hundred, the thousand mouths of this curving, undulating thing—cry out not to him, but to the universe. At the lips of particular mouths, he glimpses a myriad of tongues, long and pale and slender, each pronouncing its own syllables, filling the air with a different tone. The thing is a choir, its music a drug, and that is when he feels the gentle touch behind him, at his rump, in the small of his back, behind the knees: slender appendages unseen to him, but soft and smooth and gently implacable, draw him forward to the surface of the thing. When he touches it, he finds its flesh soft, smelling of honey and milk, the tangy reek of a lover's armpit on a hot day, the sweet warmth of a lover's mouth grasping for his own lips.

The unearthly thing twists and bends, folding itself around him, and he feels the music not only enveloping him, but passing through his own meek, tiny body. He is puny, now, enfolded by this coiling wall of flesh, and his muscles fail him as it begins to extrude countless tiny pimples, shuddering and swelling from the smooth skin between the endless singing mouths, pressing against him as the voices scream forth again from that multitude of mouths. A sort of radiant milkiness begins to leak from the swelling pimples, at first only in droplets, but soon in thick luminescent streams, warm and sweet and slippery, and he is possessed by an instinct deep, familiar, forgotten, to suckle at them and drink. Revulsion rises within him at the thought, and fear that he will drink only putrescence, pollution, but the instinct overpowers him, and he suckles at one, then another and another. The milk fills him with a calm warmth, his body suddenly seeming as distant as another galaxy, as the beginnings of the world.

The music is rasping through him now, directly, as singing tongues emerge from a dozen mouths like endless smooth fingers tapering into filaments of pure light, wrapping around him, tickling him where his flesh puckers. They encircle him, tugging and pressing and squeezing him, rubbing him as a woman might, crushing him like a bug in a machine, cradling him as a mother would. All around him, the mouths drink the milk, the music gurgling, and a blast of warm air fills the womb-like space where he hangs, suspended, naked, covered in the milky wetness, the endless untoothed mouths kissing and sucking his dark, goosepimpled flesh. His own mouth opens, and a long, warm tongue slides into it—one, then another, and another, until his mouth is full of them, wriggling and caressing his own tongue, and he must breathe through his nose or die. And what he expected to revolt him, instead fills him with a violent excitement—the almost-alcoholic fumes of the divine surging into his mouth, like milk and opiate tea and poison all at once.

His mind floods with images and sensations alien and distant—a webwork of fungal tendrils spanning all the space between the stars, singing voicelessly through its own fibers, its mycological ruminations drifting like spores among the space dust; the gloaming of a malignant red star in the distance, drifting towards the heart of the galaxy. In distant corners of the universe, gaps are widening, rifts opening and voices whispering through into the guts of the stars. Vast fungal tongues wide enough to curl around whole worlds extend through the rents, spores tumbling silently across the frigid darkness. A vast chaos of light-hunger and consciousness and gibbering thought unfurls, spreading itself out across the heavens like a plague, spreading slowly toward the Earth.

Somewhere very near by, he knows, a woman is standing in a room, her eyes closed. She is listening into the night, to the call of those otherworldly voices in the heavens, to the earth rumbling from its trackless depths. She knows he is here, and that her tenure, so wearyingly long, is finally at an end.

The tongues grasp at him, with a strange half-ferocity, fighting softly over every small appendage, pulling them this way and then that, drawing every fragment of him they can into one bright warm mouth after another, and another, the nibbling and squeezing beginning now to burn him, to make him struggle now against the softly growing panic, as a black, paralytic eternity yawns open within him.

He thinks of his yogic studies, of Shiva and Parvati atop Mt. Kailash, *lingam* in *yoni*—realizing this is also the *hieros gamos*, the same story he is living now—but to his horror he feels his body lashing out, struggling against the absoluteness of this consumption. He is losing control, feels the spasm before it hits him, waiting on the edge of his consciousness, squeezing its way through his nerves in their bloody bundles, searing and overloaded for...has it been hours? Has it only been minutes? Will he displease this god, this...goddess? If this is the *hieros gamos*, he must be the groom, so she is a goddess, is she not? And if she *is* displeased, what will happen to him? The tongues coil and twist round him like rough-skinned snakes, squeezing harder now as another mouth yawns open, and the thing seems to invert itself, so that the mouth closes with him, with the whole surface of this thing, somehow now *inside* the goddess, the mouths now ducts, the tongues now cilia on the walls of what has become a crushing maw flooded with milk and sweat and the fluids of his body as the whole of it rubs him, grinds him until he fears he shall end up a pulp. He is drowning, now, in bright sweet milk, and he loses track of *lingam* and *yoni*, or rather his whole self becomes *lingam* within *yoni*, and the spasm finally erupts through him. He shivers. He leaks a gurgling noise. *Lingam* spurts, *yoni* crushes.

He is dying, his mind blank save for the strange-colored light, save a sense of desperation as his convulsions continue, on and on for what could be hours more.

It's over, he thinks, sighing, and relaxes, waiting to be released from the grip of the goddess, or perhaps torn apart if he has displeased her.

But he is not released; the mouth does not open, does not spew him forth or chew him up, but only retains him as he calms and grows still. A bundle of tapered tongues are clinging to the inside of his mouth, probing and teasing him at the top of his throat.

A tongue tickles the edge of one of his nostrils.

And the *hieros gamos* continues, inverting: the tongues reach down his throat, probing gently. As another wave of milk floods his body, a slender tongue crawls between his legs, rubbing the pucker of his arse, and panic sets in. Bandyopadhyay shivers, unable to resist as the slick tongue slides up into him. The *lingam* becomes *yoni*, and *yoni* becomes a multitude of *lingams*. Another tongue slides into one of his nostrils, and goes fat and rigid, pumping itself into his nose with a terrifyingly frenzied urgency.

And then, the final revelation: a miniscule tongue, a wispy filamentary tentacle of almost-nothingness, reaches out from deep within the thing, probes the tip of his penis, where it is clasped, slick and soft. Bandyopadhyay screams as the tongue quickly slides into it, squirming and shivering within him; he is horrified by the ecstatic terror that begins to flood him when the slick tongue stiffens and swells, clogging the tiny passage, and then twists itself and turns from side to side within him. In a dozen disconnected rhythms, the swollen tongues ripple and squirm inside him, pumping themselves into his body, as if searching for something, some secret hidden corner where lies buried something precious and lost. The mouths drool torrents of thick, viscous milk, flooding the fleshy chamber housing this *hieros gamos*, which Bandyopadhyay begins to realize is not a mouth at all, but some kind of womb, or amniotic sac.

Eternities pass, the rigid tongues spewing into him what taste, in his mouth, like the divine substances—honey, blood, a sticky kind of liquid light, a gooey, rich almost-milk—only to retreat, replaced by other tongues, one after another. Bandyopadhyay remembers the story of Persephone now: his mind is clotted with light, with the scarlet stain of persimmon seeds, with all of the countless tongues within him now. He knows now why Persephone complies, and goes to Hades: if he resists, he will be torn apart, of that he is certain. But in surrendering, his mind is burned almost completely away, cleansed from him like a flimsy tattered fragment of fabric, and he feels madness creeping in at its edges. He holds it at bay, as best he can, by a dozen techniques gleaned from his studies: holding the empty silence within himself that he learned to build in practising yoga; executing minor theurgic wards and invocations within his mind; speaking the names to himself, again and again, though the sound of his voice is drowned out by the howling chorus of tongue-crammed mouths all around him: Demeter, Parvati, Persephone, Kali, Koré, Guan Yin, Lakshmi, Mary...

He senses feminine presences all around him, within him, as the milk grows sticky on his skin, hardening slightly. But these goddesses are nothing like this secret thing, this Mystery of Mysteries that dwells in the pit. *They* are feminine, woman-like, a complement of sorts to him, while the *thing in the pit* transcends all of that, is insatiable, inhuman and absolute—a truer picture of divinity, warm and brutal and bright and endless and void of words any human tongue could speak. *The thing in the pit is the groom* and *the bride both*, Bandopadhyay realizes, *and I am merely the wedding feast.*

And at the end of that final eternity, the fleshly tongues withdraw, all at once, gently licking him clean of the milk, the blood and light and honey. Aching in every muscle, in every gap and crevice of his body, his mind shattered, he tumbles through the warm night air, to land on in the dirt on his back, up near the edge of the pit. He is naked and still, gasping for breath and then crying out meekly: wrecked, but alive.

The Greek man—archaeologist, cultist, whatever—is there, the faint traces of a luminescent dawn visible in the distance behind him, a look of complete shock on his face.

"You have...how did you?"

Bandyopadhyay cannot speak. He merely stares dully at the Greek.

"You're the first in a hundred years to...to survive! I thought you would just..." The man is not quite so awestruck as to finish his sentence, but neither does he apologize: instead, he just reaches down and says, "Come on." When Bandyopadhyay is on his feet, the Greek strips off his own shirt and drapes it over the slender Indian's back, and wraps an arm around his shoulder, supporting the foreigner's weight. With a pious voice, he says, "It's morning, and there is someone I must... I must bring you to her."

Bandyopadhyay's legs are still a little shaky, now, and sacred fluid drips from his skin, but he stops after a few steps and turns to face the Greek amid the ruins. The Indian wobbles his head, writing a word in Sanskrit across his imagination, and tracing it in scarlet pomegranate juice. He infuses it with the radiant fluid that still rages within his mind's eye, stinking of honey and writhing like infinite tongues within him, and then, softly, he speaks the word. *Ajīvita*, he says, and the Greek's horrified face shines like the moon in the sky at dawn, a terrifying luminescence spreading across it, illuminating it more and more profoundly, until there is nothing there but whiteness, and a scream that collapses into silence.

The Greek collapses at his feet.

He stands for a moment, stunned, half unable to believe that the evocation worked this time. He casts his eyes back toward where the pit had been, before turning again toward the rising sun. He looks down at the shirtless, white-faced body. He will leave it where it fell, as a warning.

Then Bandyopadhyay turns, searching the sky for light, for those distinct, tubular shapes of the divine form, multifarious above as when he had glimpsed them the night before. But there are only clouds above now, and the rosy-fingered dawn, and the sound of morning traffic and cicadas beginning their rasping symphonies again, and the stink of profane things—paint factories, his own stale sweat, the faintest dull aroma of the dust that clings implacably, that dust of the plain, still, voiceless earth.

He turns in the direction the Greek had begun to lead him. He knows, somehow, where to go, and what waits there for him. A lifetime of adoration, of worship, of longing to return to that subterranean womb. Beyond *lingam* and *yoni*, now, beyond life and death, he is Hierophant, the hand above the earth which feeds the teeming mouth beneath, *mystes* turned *mystagogus*.

At last, his roaming is over: he has found his way, finally, home to this place on the verge of the Elysian fields, those strange other worlds beyond the clefts in space, from which flow the unknowable colors. Here he stands, with the divine beneath his very feet, whispering his name, crying out to him to complete the rite with voices so innumerable and forceful he fears his mind may crumble even to hear it any longer, and yet he delights in the pain. No book ever gave him such relief; no translation, such insight.

He is home, a home that will be his soon, once he completes the marriage rite by performing the *nekuia*; when the ground is speckled with the milk, and honey, and blood, like in the poem, and he has taken his predecessor's place. She will bare her neck to him, as her predecessor bared his neck to her. She will sing as the blood pours out, until she can sing no more.

They will sing together, in adoration of the Mysteries.

The LITANY of EARTH

Ruthanna Emrys

AFTER A YEAR IN SAN FRANCISCO, my legs grew strong again. A hill and a half lay between the bookstore where I found work and the apartment I shared with the Kotos. Every morning and evening I walked, breathing mist and rain into my desert-scarred lungs, and every morning the walk was a little easier. Even at the beginning, when my feet ached all day from the unaccustomed strain, it was a hill and a half that I hadn't been permitted for seventeen years.

In the evenings, the radio told what I had missed: an earth-spanning war, and atrocities in Europe to match and even exceed what had been done to both our peoples. We did not ask, the Kotos and I, whether our captors too would eventually be called to justice. The Japanese American community, for the most part, was trying to put the camps behind them. And it was not the way of my folk—who had grown resigned to the camps long before the Kotos' people were sent to join us, and who no longer had a community on land—to dwell on impossibilities.

That morning, I had received a letter from my brother. Caleb didn't write often, and hearing from him was equal parts relief and uncomfortable reminder. His grammar was good, but his handwriting and spelling revealed the paucity of his lessons. He had written:

The town is a ruin, but not near enouff of one. Houses still stand; even a few windos are whole. It has all been looked over most carefully long ago, but I think forgotten or ignorred since.

And:

I looked through our library, and those of other houses, but there is not a book or torn page left on the shelves. I have saugt permisson to look throuh the collecton at Miskatonic, but they are putting me off. I very much fear that the most importent volumes were placed in some government warehouse to be forgotten—as we were.

So, our family collections were still lost. I remembered the feel of the old pages, my father leaning over me, long fingers tracing a difficult passage as he explained its meaning—and my mother, breaking in with some simple suggestion that cut to the heart of it. Now, the only books I had to work with were the basic texts and a single children's spellbook in the store's backroom collection. The texts, in fact, belonged to Charlie—my boss—and I bartered my half-remembered childhood Enochian and R'lyehn for access.

Charlie looked up and frowned as the bells announced my arrival. He had done that from the first time I came in to apply, and so far as I knew gave all his customers the same glare.

"Miss Marsh."

I closed my eyes and breathed in the paper-sweet dust. "I'm not late, Mr. Day."

"We need to finish the inventory this morning. You can start with the westerns."

I stuck my purse behind the counter and headed back toward the piles of spine-creased Edgar Rice Burroughs and Zane Grey. "What I like about you," I said honestly, "is that you don't pretend to be civil."

"And dry off first." But no arguments, by now, that I ought to carry an umbrella or wear a jacket. No questions about why I liked the damp and chill, second only to the company of old books. Charlie wasn't unimaginative, but he kept his curiosity to himself.

I spent the rest of the morning shelving. Sometimes I would read a passage at random, drinking in the impossible luxury of ink organized into meaningful patterns. Very occasionally I would bring one forward and read a bit aloud to Charlie, who would harumph at me and continue with his work, or read me a paragraph of his own.

By midafternoon I was holding down the register while Charlie did something finicky and specific with the cookbooks. The bells jangled. A man poked his head in, sniffed cautiously, and made directly for me.

"Excuse me. I'm looking for books on the occult—for research." He smiled, a salesman's too-open expression, daring me to disapprove. I showed him to the shelf where we kept Crowley and other such nonsense, and returned to the counter frowning thoughtfully.

After a few minutes, he returned. "None of that is quite what I'm looking for. Do you keep anything more...esoteric?"

"I'm afraid not, sir. What you see is what we have."

He leaned across the counter. His scent, ordinary sweat and faint cologne, insinuated itself against me, and I stepped back out of reach. "Maybe something in a storage room? I'm sure you must have more than these turn-of-the-century fakers. Some Al-Hazred, say? Prinn's *Vermis*?"

I tried not to flinch. I knew the look of the old families, and he had none of it—tall and dark-haired and thin-faced, conventional attractiveness marred by nothing more than a somewhat square nose. Nor was he cautious in revealing his familiarity with the Aeonist canon, as Charlie had been. He was either stupid, or playing with me.

"I've never heard of either," I said. "We don't specialize in esoterica; I'm afraid you'd better try another store."

"I don't think that's necessary." He drew himself straighter, and I took another step back. He smiled again, in a way I thought was intended to be friendly, but seemed rather the bare-toothed threat of an ape. "Miss Aphra Marsh. I know you're familiar with these things, and I'm sure we can help each other."

I held my ground and gave my mother's best glare. "You have me mistaken, sir. If you are not in the store to purchase goods that we actually have, I strongly suggest that you look elsewhere."

He shrugged and held out his hands. "Perhaps later."

Charlie limped back to the counter as the door rang the man's departure. "Customer?"

"No." My hands were trembling, and I clasped them behind my back. "He wanted to know about your private shelf. Charlie, I don't like him. I don't trust him."

He frowned again and glanced toward the employees-only door. "Thief?"

That would have been best, certainly. My pulse fluttered in my throat. "Well informed, if so."

Charlie must have seen how hard I was holding myself. He found the metal thermos and offered it silently. I shook my head, and with a surge of dizziness found myself on the floor. I wrapped my arms around my knees and continued to shake my head at whatever else might be offered.

"He might be after the books," I forced out at last. "Or he might be after us."

He crouched next to me, moving slowly with his bad knee and the stiffness of joints beginning to admit mortality. "For having the books?"

I shook my head again. "Yes. Or for being the sort of people who would have them." I stared at my interlaced fingers, long and bony, as though they might be thinking about growing extra joints. There was no way to explain the idea I had, that the smiling man might come back with more men, and guns, and vans that locked in the back. And probably he was only a poorly spoken dabbler, harmless. "He knew my name."

Charlie pulled himself up and into a chair, settling with a grunt. "I don't suppose he could have been one of those Yith you told me about?"

I looked up, struck by the idea. I had always thought of the Great Race as solemn and wise, and meeting one was supposed to be very lucky. But they were also known to be arrogant and abrupt, when they wanted something. It was a nice thought. "I don't think so. They have phrases, secret ways of making themselves known to people who would recognize them. I'm afraid he was just a man."

"Well." Charlie got to his feet. "No help for it unless he comes back. Do you need to go home early?"

That was quite an offer, coming from Charlie, and I couldn't bear the thought that I looked like I needed it. I eased myself off the floor, the remaining edge of fear making me slow and clumsy. "Thank you. I'd rather stay here. Just warn me if you see him again."

The first change in my new life, also heralded by a customer...

It is not yet a month since my return to the world. I am still weak, my skin sallow from malnourishment and dehydration. After my first look in a good mirror, I have shaved my brittle locks to the quick, and the new are growing in ragged, but thick and rich and dark like my mother's. My hair as an adult woman, which I have never seen 'til now.

I am shelving when a familiar phrase stings my ears. Hope and danger, tingling together as I drift forward, straining to hear more.

The blond man is trying to sell Charlie a copy of the *Book of the Grey People*, but it soon becomes apparent that he knows little but the title. I should be more cautious than I am next, should think more carefully about what I reveal. But I like Charlie, his gruffness and his honesty and the endless difference between him and everything I have hated or loved. I don't like to see him taken in.

The blond man startles when I appear by his shoulder, but when I pull the tome over to flip the pages, he tries to regroup. "Now just a minute here, young lady. This book is valuable."

I cannot imagine that I truly look less than my thirty years. "This book is a fake. Is this supposed to be Enochian?"

"Of course it's Enochian. Let me—"

"Ab-kar-rak al-laz-kar-nef—" I sound out the paragraph in front of me. "This was written by someone who had heard Enochian once, and vaguely recalled the sound of it. It's gibberish. And in the wrong alphabet, besides. And the binding..." I run my hand over it and shudder. "The binding is real skin. Which makes this a very expensive fake for *someone*, but the price has already been paid. Take this abomination away."

Charlie looks at me as the blond man leaves. I draw myself up, determined to make the best of it. I can always work at the laundromat with Anna.

"You know Enochian?" he asks. I'm startled by the gentleness—and the hope. I can hardly lie about it now, but I don't give more than the bare truth.

"I learned it as a child."

His eyes sweep over my face; I hold myself impassive against his judgment. "I believe you keep secrets, and keep them well," he says at last. "I don't plan to pry. But I want to show you one of mine, if you can keep that too."

This isn't what I was expecting. But he might learn more about me, someday, as much as I try to hide. And when that happens, I'll need a reason to trust him. "I promise."

"Come on back." He turns the door sign before leading me to the storage room that has been locked all the weeks I've worked here.

I stayed as late as I could, until I realized that if someone was asking after me, the Kotos might be in danger as well. I didn't want to call, unsure if the phone lines would be safe. All the man had done was talk to me—I might never see him again. Even so, I would be twitching for weeks. You don't forget the things that can develop from other people's small suspicions.

The night air was brisk, chilly by most people's standards. The moon watched over the city, soft and gibbous, outlines blurred by San Francisco's ubiquitous mist. Sounds echoed closer than their objects. I might have been swimming, sensations carried effortlessly on ocean currents. I licked salt from my lips, and prayed. I wished I could break the habit, but I wished more, still, that just once it would work.

"Miss Marsh!" The words pierced the damp night. I breathed clean mist and kept walking. *Iä, Cthulhu...*

"Please, Miss Marsh, I just need a moment of your time." The words were polite enough, but the voice was too confident. I walked faster, and strained my ears for his approach. Soft soles would not tap, but a hissing squelch marked every step on the wet sidewalk. I could not look back; I could not run: either would be an admission of guilt. He would chase me, or put a bullet in my skull.

"You have me mistaken," I said loudly. The words came as a sort of croak.

I heard him speed up, and then he was in front of me, mist clinging to his tall form. Perforce, I stopped. I wanted to escape, or call for help, but I could not imagine either.

"What do you want, sir?" The stiff words came more easily this time. It occurred to me belatedly that if he did not know what I was, he might try to force himself on me, as the soldiers sometimes had with the Japanese girls in the camp. I couldn't bring myself to fear the possibility; he moved like a different kind of predator.

"I'm sorry," he said. "I'm afraid we may have gotten off to a bad start, earlier. I'm Ron Spector; I'm with the FBI—"

He started to offer a badge, but the confirmation of my worst fears released me from my paralysis. I lashed out with one newly strong leg and darted to the side. I had intended to race home and warn the Kotos, but instead he caught his balance and grabbed my arm. I turned and grappled, scratching and pulling, all the time aware that my papa had died fighting this way. I expected the deadly shot at any moment, and struggled while I could. But my arms were weaker than Papa's, and even my legs were not what they should have been.

Gradually, I realized that Spector was only trying to hold me off, not fighting for his life, nor even for mine. He kept repeating my name, and at last:

"Please, Miss Marsh! I'm not trained for this!" He pushed me back again, and grunted as my nails drew blood on his unprotected wrist. "Please! I don't mean you any harm; I just want to talk for five minutes. Five minutes, I promise, and then you can stay or go as you please!"

My panic could not sustain itself, and I stilled at last. Even then, I was afraid that given the chance, he would clap me in irons. But we held our tableau, locked hand to wrist. His mortal pulse flickered mouse-like against my fingertips, and I was sure he could feel mine roaring like the tide.

"If I let you go, will you listen?"

I breathed in strength from the salt fog. "Five minutes, you said."

"Yes." He released me, and rubbed the skin below his wristwatch. "I'm sorry, I should have been more circumspect. I know what you've been through."

"Do you." I controlled my shaking with effort. I was a Marsh; I would not show weakness to an enemy. They had drunk deep of it already.

He looked around and took a careful seat on one of the stones bordering a nearby yard. It was too short for him, so that his knees bent upward when he sat. He leaned forward: a praying mantis in a black suit.

"Most religions consist largely of good people trying to get by. No matter what names they worship, or what church they go to, or what language they pray in. Will you agree with me on this much?"

I folded my arms and waited.

"And every religion has its fanatics, who are willing to do terrible things in the name of their god. No one is immune." His lips quirked. "It's a failing of humanity, not of any particular sect."

"I'll grant you that. What of it?" I counted seconds in drips of water. I could almost imagine the dew clinging to my skin as a shield.

He shrugged and smiled. I didn't like how easy he could be, with his wrist still stinking of blood. "If you grant me that, you're already several steps ahead of the U.S. government, just post–World War I. In the twenties, they had run-ins with a couple of nasty Aeonist groups. There was one cult down in Louisiana that had probably never seen an original bit of the canon, but they had their ideas. Sacrificial corpses hanging from trees, the whole nine yards." He glanced at me, checking for some reaction. I did not grant it.

"Not exactly representative, but we got the idea that was normal. In '26, the whole religion were declared enemies of the state, and we started looking out for anyone who said the wrong names on Sunday night, or had the wrong statues in their churches. You know where it goes from there."

I did, and wondered how much he really knew. It was strange, nauseating, to hear the justifications, even as he tried to hold them at a distance.

"It won't shock you," he continued, "to know that Innsmouth wasn't the only place that suffered. Eventually, it occurred to the government that they might have overgeneralized, but it took a long time for changes to go through. Now we're starting to have people like me, who actually study Aeonist culture and try to separate out the bad guys, but it's been a long time coming."

I held myself very still through his practiced speech. "If this is by way of an apology, Mr. Spector, you can drown in it. What you did was beyond the power of any apology."

"Doubtless we owe you one anyway, if we can find a decent way of making it. But I'm afraid I've been sent to speak with you for practical reasons." He cleared his throat and shifted his knees. "As you may imagine, when the government went hunting Aeonists, it was much easier to find good people, minding their own business in small towns, than cultists well-practiced in conspiracy and murder. The bad guys tend to be better at hiding, after all. And at the same time, we weren't trying to recruit people who knew anything useful about the subject— after a while, few would have been willing even if we went looking. So now, as with the Japanese American community, we find ourselves shorthanded, ignorant, and having angered the people least likely to be a danger to the country."

My eye sockets ached. "I cannot believe that you are trying to recruit me."

"I'm afraid that's exactly what I'm doing. I could offer—"

"Your five minutes are up, sir." I walked past him, biting back anything else I might say, or think. The anger worked its way into my shoulders, and my legs, and the rush of my blood.

"Miss Marsh!"

Against my better judgment, I stopped and turned back. I imagined what I must look like to him. Bulging eyes; wide mouth; long, bony legs and fingers. "The Innsmouth look," when there was an Innsmouth. Did it signal danger to him? Something more than human, or less? Perhaps he saw just an ugly woman, someone whose reactions he could dismiss until he heard what he wanted.

Then I would speak clearly.

"Mr. Spector, I have no interest in being an enemy of the state. The state is larger than I. But nor will I be any part of it. And if you insist, you will listen to why. *The state* stole nearly two decades of my life. *The state* killed my father, and locked the rest of my family away from anything they thought might give us strength. Salt water. Books. Knowledge. One by one, they destroyed us. My mother began her metamorphosis. Allowed the ocean, she might have lived until the sun burned to ashes. They took her away. We know they studied us at such times, to better know the process. To better know how to hurt us. You must imagine the details, as I have. They never returned the bodies. Nothing has been given back to us.

"Now, ask me again."

He bent his head at last. Not in shame, I thought, but listening. Then he spoke softly. "The state is not one entity. It is *changing*. And when it changes, it's good for everyone. The people you could help us stop are truly hurting others. And the ones being hurt know nothing of what was done to your family. Will you hold the actions of a few against them? Should more families suffer because yours did?"

I reminded myself that, after humanity faded and died, a great insectoid civilization would live in these hills. After that, the Sareeav, with their pseudopods and strange sculptures. Therefore, I could show patience. "I will do what I can for suffering on my own."

More quietly: "If you helped us, even on one matter, I might be able to find out what really happened to your mother."

The guilt showed plainly on his face as soon as he said it, but I still had to turn away. "I cannot believe that even after her death, you would dare hold my mother hostage for my good behavior. You can keep her body, and your secrets." And in R'lyehn, because we had been punished for using it in the camps, I added, "And if they hang your corpse from a tree, I will kiss the ground beneath it." Then, fearful that he might do more, or say more, I ran.

I kicked off my shoes, desperate for speed. My feet slapped the wet ground. I could not hear whether Spector followed me. I was still too weak, as weak as I had been as a child, but I was taller, and faster, and the fog wrapped me and hid me and sped me on my flight.

Some minutes later I ducked into a side drive. Peering out, I saw no one following me. Then I let myself gasp: deep, shuddering breaths. I wanted him dead. I wanted them all dead, as I had for seventeen years. Probably some of them were: they were only ordinary humans, with creaking joints and rivulet veins. I could be patient.

I came in barefoot to the Kotos. Mama Rei was in the kitchen. She put down her chopping knife, and held me while I shook. Then Anna took my hand and drew me over to the table. The others hovered nearby,

Neko looking concerned and Kevin sucking his thumb. He reminded me so very much of Caleb.

"What happened?" asked Anna, and I told them everything, trying to be calm and clear. They had to know.

Mama Rei tossed a handful of onions into the pan and started on the peppers. She didn't look at me, but she didn't need to. "Aphra-chan—Kappa-sama—what do you think he wants?"

I started to rub my face, then winced. Spector's blood, still on my nails, cut through the clean smell of frying onion. "I don't know. Perhaps only what he said, but his masters will certainly be angry when he fails to recruit me. He might seek ways to put pressure on me. It's not safe. I'm sorry."

"I don't want to leave," said Neko. "We just got here." I closed my eyes hard against the sting.

"We won't leave," said Mama Rei. "We are trying to build a decent life here, and I won't be scared away from it. Neither will you, Aphra-chan. This government man can only do so much to us, without a law to say he can lock us up."

"There was no law countenancing the things done to my family," I said.

"Times have changed," she said firmly. "People are watching, now."

"They took your whole town," said Anna, almost gently. "They can't take all of San Francisco, can they, Mama?"

"Of course not. We will live our lives, and you will all go to work and school tomorrow, and we will be careful. That is all."

There was no arguing with Mama Rei, and I didn't really want to. I loved the life I had, and if I lost it again, well... the sun would burn to ash soon enough, and then it would make little difference whether I had a few months of happiness here, or a few years. I fell asleep praying.

One expects the storage room of a bookstore to hold more books. And it does. Books in boxes, books on shelves, books piled on the floor and the birch table with uneven legs. And one bookshelf more solid than the others, leaves and vines carved into dark wood. The sort that one buys for too much money, to hold something that feels like it deserves the respect.

And on the shelves, my childhood mixed with dross. I hold up my hand, afraid to touch, to run it across the titles, a finger's breadth away. I fear that they too will change to gibberish. Some of them already are. Some are titles I know to have been written by charlatans, or fakes as obvious as the blond man's *Grey People*. And some are real.

"Where did you get these?"

"At auction. At estate sales. From people who come in offering to sell, or other stores that don't know what they have. To tell the truth, I don't entirely either, for some of them. You might have a better idea?"

I pull down a *Necronomicon* with shaking hands, the one of his three that looks real. The inside page is thankfully empty—no dedication, no list of family names. No chance of learning whether it ever belonged to someone I knew. I read the first page, enough to recognize the over-poetic Arabic, and put it back before my eyes can tear up. I take another, this one in true Enochian.

"Why buy them, if you can't read them?"

"Because I might be able to, someday. Because I might be able to learn something, even with a word or two. Because I want to learn magic, if you must know, and this is the closest I can come." His glare dares me to scoff.

I hold out the book I've been cradling. "You could learn from this one, you know. It's a child's introductory text. I learned a little from it, myself, before I... lost access to my library." My glare dares him to ask. He doesn't intrude on my privacy, no more than I laugh at what he's revealed. "I don't know enough to teach you properly. But if you let me share your books, I'll help you learn as best I can." He nods, and I turn my head aside so my tears don't fall on the text—or where he can see.

I returned to work the next day, wearing shoes borrowed from neighbors. My feet were far too big for anything the Kotos could lend me. Anna walked me partway before turning off for the laundromat— her company more comfort than I cared to admit.

I had hovered by the sink before breakfast, considering what to do about the faint smudge of Spector's blood. In the end, I washed it off.

A government agent, familiar with the Aeonist canons, might well know how to detect the signs if I used it against him.

Despite my fears, that day was a quiet one, full of customers asking for westerns and romances and textbooks. The next day was the same, and the day after that, and three weeks passed with the tension between my shoulder blades the only indication that something was amiss.

At the end of those three weeks, he came again. His body language had changed: a little hunched, a little less certain. I stiffened, but did not run. Charlie looked up from the stack of incoming books, and gave the requisite glare.

"That's him," I murmured.

"Ah." The glare deepened. "You're not welcome here. Get out of my store, and don't bother my employees again."

Spector straightened, recovering a bit of his old arrogance. "I have something for Miss Marsh. Then I'll go."

"Whatever you have to offer, I don't want it. You heard Mr. Day: you're trespassing."

He ducked his head. "I found your mother's records. I'm not offering them in exchange for anything. You were right, that wasn't... wasn't honorable. Once you've seen them—if you want to see them—I'll go."

I held out my hand. "Very well. I'll take them. And then you will leave."

He held on to the thick folder. "I'm sorry, Miss Marsh. I've got to stay with them. They aren't supposed to be out of the building, and I'm not supposed to have them right now. I'll be in serious trouble if I lose them."

I didn't care if he got in trouble, and I didn't want to see what was in the folder. But it was my mother's only grave. "Mr. Day," I said quietly. "I would like a few minutes of privacy, if you please."

Charlie took a box and headed away, but paused. "You just shout if this fellow gives you any trouble." He gave Spector another glare before heading into the stacks—I suspected not very far.

Spector handed me the folder. I opened it, cautiously, between the cash register and a short stack of Agatha Christie novels. For a moment I closed my eyes, fixing my mother's living image in my mind. I remembered her singing a sacred chanty in the kitchen, arguing with shopkeepers, kneeling in the wet sand at Solstice. I remembered one of our neighbors crying in our sitting room after her husband's boat was lost in a storm, telling her, "Your faith goes all the way to the depths. Some of us aren't so lucky."

"I'm sorry," Spector said quietly. "It's ugly."

They had taken her deeper into the desert, to an experimental station. They had caged her. They had given her weights to lift, testing her strength. They had starved her for days, testing her endurance. They had cut her, confusing their mythologies, with iron and silver, noting healing times. They had washed her once with seawater, then fresh, then scrubbed her with dry salt. After that, they had refused her all contact with water, save a minimum to drink. Then not even that. For the whole of sixty-seven days, they carefully recorded her pulse, her skin tone, and the distance between her eyes. Perhaps in some vague way also interested in our culture, they copied, faithfully, every word she spoke.

Not one sentence was a prayer.

There were photos, both from the experiments and the autopsy afterward. I did not cry. It seemed extravagant to waste salt water so freely.

"Thank you," I said quietly, closing the folder, bile burning the back of my throat. He bowed his head.

"My mother came to the states young." He spoke deliberately, neither rushing to share nor stumbling over his apparent honesty. Anything else, I would have felt justified interrupting. "Her sister stayed in Poland. She was a bit older, and she had a sweetheart. I have files on her, too. She survived. She's in a hospital in Israel, and sometimes she can feed herself." He stopped, took a deep breath, shook his head. "I can't think of anything that would convince me to work for the new German government—no matter how different it is from the old. I'm sorry I asked."

He took the folder and turned away.

"Wait." I should not have said it. He'd probably staged the whole thing. But it was a far more thoughtful manipulation than the threats I had expected—and I found myself afraid to go on ignoring my enemies. "I will not work for you. But tell me about these frightening new Aeonists."

Whatever—if anything—I eventually chose to pass on to Spector, I realized that I very much wanted to meet them. For all the Kotos' love and comfort, and for all Charlie's eager learning, I still missed Innsmouth. These mortals might be the closest I could come to home.

"Why do you want to learn this?" Though I doubt Charlie knows, it's a ritual question. There is no ritual answer.

"I don't . . ." He glares, a habit my father would have demanded he break before pursuing the ancient scholarship. "Some things don't go into words easily, all right? It's . . . it feels like what *should* be in books, I suppose. They should all be able to change the world. At least a little."

I nod. "That's a good answer. Some people think that 'power' is a good answer, and it isn't. The power that can be found in magic is less than what you get from a gun, or a badge, or a bomb." I pause. "I'm trying to remember all the things I need to tell you, now, at the beginning. What magic is *for* is understanding. Knowledge. And it won't work until you know how little that gets you.

"*Sharhlyda*—Aeonism—is a bit like a religion. But this isn't the Bible—most of the things I'm going to tell you are things we have records of: histories older than man, and sometimes the testimony of those who lived them. The gods you can take or leave, but the history is real.

"All of man's other religions place him at the center of creation. But man is nothing—a fraction of the life that will walk the Earth. Earth is nothing—a tiny world that will die with its sun. The sun is one of trillions where life flowers, and wants to live, and dies. And between the suns is an endless vast darkness that dwarfs them, through which life can travel only by giving up that wanting, by losing itself. Even that darkness will eventually die. In such a universe, knowledge is the stub of a candle at dusk."

"You make it all sound so cheerful."

"It's honest. What our religion tells us, the part that is a religion, is that the gods created life to try and make meaning. It's ultimately hopeless, and even gods die, but the effort is real. Will always have been real, even when everything is over and no one remembers."

Charlie looks dubious. I didn't believe it, either, when I first started learning. And I was too young then to find it either frightening or comforting.

I thought about what Mr. Spector had told me, and about what I might do with the information. Eventually I found myself, unofficially and entirely on my own recognizance, in a better part of the city, past sunset, at the door of a home rather nicer than the Kotos'. It was no mansion by any imagining, but it was long lived-in and well kept up: two stories of brick and Spanish tile roof, with juniper guarding the façade. The door was painted a cheerful yellow, but the knocker was a fantastical wrought-iron creature that reminded me painfully of home. I lifted the cold metal and rapped sharply. Then I waited, shivering.

The man who opened the door looked older than Charlie. His gray hair frizzed around the temples and ears, otherwise slick as a seal. Faint lines creased his cheeks. He frowned at me. I hoped I had the right address.

"My name is Aphra Marsh," I said. "Does that mean anything to you? I understand that some in this house still follow the old ways."

He started, enough to tell me that he recognized my family's name. He shuffled back a little, but then leaned forward. "Where did you hear such a thing?"

"My family have their ways. May I enter?"

He stepped aside to let me in, in too reluctant a fashion to be truly gallant. His pupils widened between narrowed eyelids, and he licked his lips.

"What do you want, my lady?"

Ignoring the question for the moment, I stepped inside. The foyer, and what I could see of the parlor, looked pedestrian but painfully familiar. Dark wood furniture, much of it bookshelves, contrasted with leaf-green walls. Yet it was all a bit shabby—not quite as recently dusted or mended as would have satisfied my mother's pride. A year ago, it might have been the front room of any of the better houses in Innsmouth. Now... I wondered what my family home had looked like, in the years after my mother was no longer there to take pride in it. I put the thought forcibly out of my mind.

"... in the basement," he was saying. "Would you like to see?"

I ran my memory back through the last seconds, and discovered that he was, in fact, offering to show me where they practiced "the old ways." "I would. But an introduction might be in order first?"

"My apologies, my lady. I am Oswin Wilder. High priest here, although probably not a very traditional one by your standards."

"I make no judgment." And I smiled at him in a way that suggested I might well do so later. It was strange. In Innsmouth, non-Sharhlyd outsiders had looked on us with fear and revulsion—even the Sharhlyd who were not of our kind, mostly the nervously misanthropic academics at Miskatonic, treated us with suspicion. Respect was usually subordinated to rivalries over the proper use of ancient texts. The few mortal humans who shared both our town and our faith had deferred openly, but without this taint of resentment.

He led me down solid wooden steps. I half expected a hidden sub-basement or a dungeon—I think he must have wanted one—but he had worked with the home he already had. Beyond the bare flagstone at the foot of the stairs, he had merely added a raised level of dark tile, painted with sigils and patterns. I recognized a few, but suspected more of being his own improvisations. At the far end of the room, candles flickered on a cloth-covered table. I approached, moving carefully around the simple stone altar in the center.

On the table sat a devotional statue of Cthulhu. I hardly noticed the quality of the carving or the material, although my childhood priest would have had something to say about both. But my childhood was long discarded, and the display struck my adult doubts with forgotten force. Heedless of the man behind me, I knelt. The flickering light gave a wet sheen to tentacles and limbs, and I could almost imagine again that they were reaching to draw me in and keep me safe. Where the statue in Innsmouth's church had depicted the god with eyes closed, to represent the mysteries of the deep, this one's eyes were open, black and fathomless. I returned the gaze, refusing to bow my head.

Have you been waiting for us? Do you regret what happened? With all your aeons, did you even notice that Innsmouth was gone? Or did you just wonder why fewer people came to the water?

Are you listening, now? Were you ever there to listen?

More tears, I realized too late—not something I would have chosen for the priest to see. But I flicked a drop of my salt water onto the statue, and whispered the appropriate prayer. I found it oddly comforting. My mother, old-fashioned, had kept a jar of seawater on the counter for washing tear-streaked faces, and brought it to temple once a month. But I had still given my tears to the god when I didn't want her fussing, or was trying to hide a fight with my brother.

We were near the ocean now. Perhaps the Kotos could spare a jar.

My musings were interrupted by the creak of the basement door and a tremulous alto. "Oz? I knocked, but no one answered—are you down here?"

"Mildred, yes. Come on down; we have a guest."

Full skirts, garnet red, descended, and as she came closer I saw a woman bearing all my mother's remembered dignity. She had the air of magnificence that fortunate mortals gained with age; her wrinkles and gray-streaked hair only gave the impression of deliberate artistic choices. I stood and ducked my head politely. She looked me over, thin-lipped.

"Mil—Miss Marsh," said Wilder. "Allow me to introduce Mildred Bergman. Mildred, this is Miss Aphra Marsh." He paused dramatically, and her frown deepened.

"And what is she doing in our sanctum?"

"Miss *Marsh*," he repeated.

"Anyone can claim a name. Even such an illustrious one." I winced, then lifted my chin. There was no reason for me to feel hurt: her doubt should be no worse a barrier than Wilder's nervous pride.

Taking a candle from the altar for light—and with a whisper of thanks to Cthulhu for the loan—I stepped toward her. She stood her ground. "Look at me."

She looked me up and down, making a show of it. Her eyes stayed narrow, and if I had studied long enough to hear thoughts, and done the appropriate rites, I was sure I would have heard it. *Anyone can be ugly.*

Wilder moved to intervene. "This is silly. We have no reason to doubt her. And she found us on her own. She must have some knowledge of the old arts: we don't exactly put our address in the classifieds. Let it go and give her a chance to prove herself."

Bergman sniffed and shrugged. Moving faster than I would have expected, she plucked the candle from my hand and replaced it on the table. "As high priest, it is of course at your discretion what newcomers must do to join the elect. The others will be here soon; we'll see what they think of your guest."

I blinked at her. "I'll wait, then." I turned my back and knelt again at the god's table. I would not let her see my rage at her dismissal, or the fear that the gesture of defiance cost me.

The first and most basic exercise in magic is looking at oneself. Truly looking, truly seeing—and I am afraid. I cannot quite persuade myself that the years in the camp haven't stolen something vital. After doing this simple thing, I will know.

I sit opposite Charlie on the plain wood floor of the storage room. He has dragged over a rag rug and the cushion from a chair for his knees, but I welcome the cool solidity. Around us I have drawn a first-level seal in red chalk, and between us placed two bowls of salt water and two knives. I have walked him through this in the book, told him what to expect, as well as I am able. I remember my father, steady and patient as he explained the rite. I may be more like my mother—impatient with beginners' mistakes, even my own.

I lead him through a grounding: tell him to imagine the sea in his veins, his body as a torrent of blood and breath. I simplify the imagery I learned as a child. He has no metamorphosis to imagine, no ancestors to tell him how those things feel under the weight of the depths. But he closes his eyes and breathes, and I imagine it as wind on a hot day. He is a man of the air, after all. I must tell him the Litany so he will know what that means, and perhaps he will make a new grounding that fits.

Bodies and minds settled, we begin the chant. His pronunciation is poor, but this is a child's exercise and designed for a leader and a stumbling apprentice. The words rise, bearing the rhythm of wind and wave and the slow movement of the earth. Still chanting, I lift the knife, and watch Charlie follow my lead. I wash the blade in salt water and prick my finger. The sting is familiar, welcome. I let a drop of my blood fall into the bowl, swirling and spreading and fading into clarity. I have just enough time to see that Charlie has done the same before the room too fades, and my inward perceptions turn clear.

I am inside myself, seeing with my blood rather than my eyes. I am exquisitely aware of my body, and its power. My blood *is* a torrent. It is a river emptying into the ocean; it thunders through me, a cacophony of rapids and white water. I travel with it, checking paths I have not trod for eighteen years. I find them surprisingly in order. I should have known, watching mortals age while my hard-used joints still moved easily—but that river still carries its healing force, still sweeps illnesses and aches from the banks where they try to cling. Still reshapes what it touches, patiently and steadily. Still carries all the markers of a healthy child who will someday, still, go into the water. I remember my mother telling me, smiling, that my blood knew already the form I would someday wear.

I am basking in the feel of myself, loving my body for the first time in years, when everything changes. Just for a moment, I am aware of my skin, and a touch on my arm.

"Miss Marsh, are you okay?"

And now I remember that one learns to stay inside longer with practice, and that I entirely neglected to warn Charlie against touching me. And then I am cast out of my river, and into another.

I've never tried this with anyone outside my own people. Charlie's river is terribly weak—more like a stream, in truth. It has little power, and detritus has made it narrow and shallow. Where my body is yearning toward the ocean, his has already begun to dry out. His blood, too, knows the form he will someday wear.

He must now be seeing me as intimately.

I force the connection closed, saying the words that end the rite as quickly as I dare. I come to, a little dizzy, swaying.

Charlie looks far more shaken. "That... that was real. That was magic."

And I can only feel relief. Of course, the strangeness of his first spell must overwhelm any suspicion over the differences in our blood. At least for now.

Wilder's congregation trickled in over the next hour. They were male and female, robed richly or simply, but all with an air of confidence that suggested old families used to mortal power. They murmured when

Wilder introduced them to me; some whispered more with Bergman afterward.

It only seemed like an endless aeon until they at last gathered in a circle. Wilder stood before the table, facing the low altar, and raised his arms. The circle quieted, till only their breath and the rustling of skirts and robes moved the air.

"Iä, iä, Cthulhu thtagn..." His accent was beyond abominable, but the prayer was familiar. After the fourth smoothly spoken mispronunciation, I realized that he must have learned the language entirely from books. While I had been denied wisdom writ solid in ink, he had been denied a guiding voice. Knowing he would not appreciate it now, I kept my peace. Even the mangled words were sweet.

The congregants gave their responses at the appropriate points, though many of them stumbled, and a few muttered nonsense rather than the proper words. They had learned from Wilder, some more newly than others. Many leaned forward, pupils dilated and mouths gaping with pleasure. Bergman's shoulders held the tension of real fervor, but her lids were narrowed as she avidly watched the reactions she would not show herself. Her eyes met mine and her mouth twitched.

I remembered my mother, her self-contained faith a complement to my father's easy affections. Bergman had the start of such faith, though she still seemed too conscious of her self-control.

After several minutes of call and response, Wilder knelt and took a golden necklet from where it had been hidden under the folds of the tablecloth. It was none of the work of my people—only a simple set of linked squares, with some abstract tentacular pattern carved in each one. It was as like the ornate bas-relief and wirework necklace-crowns of the deep as the ritual was like my childhood church. Wilder lifted it so that all could see, and Bergman stood before him. He switched abruptly to English: no translation that I recognized, presumably his own invention.

"Lady, wilt thou accept the love of Shub-Nigaroth? Wilt thou shine forth the wonders of life eternal for our mortal eyes?"

Bergman lifted her chin. "I shall. I am her sworn daughter, and the beloved of the Gods: let all welcome and return their terrible and glorious love."

Wilder placed the chain around her neck. She turned to face the congregation, and he continued, now hidden behind her: "Behold the glory of the All-Mother!"

"Iä Cthulhu! Iä Shub-Nigaroth!"

"Behold the dance in darkness! Behold the life that knows not death!"

"Iä! Iä!"

"Behold the secret ever hidden from the sun! See it—breathe it— take it within you!"

At this the congregation fell silent, and I stumbled over a swallowed shout of joy. The words were half nonsense, but half closer to the spirit of my remembered services than anything Wilder had pulled from his books. Bergman took from the table a knife, and a chalice full of some dark liquid. As she turned to place it on the altar, the scent of plain red wine wafted to my nostrils. She pricked her finger and squeezed a drop of blood into the cup.

As we passed the chalice from hand to hand, the congregants each sipped reverently. They closed their eyes and sighed at private visions, or stared into the wine wondering before relinquishing it to the next. Yet when it came around to me, I tasted only wine. With time and space for my own art, I might have learned from it any secrets hidden in Bergman's blood—but there was no magic here, only its trappings.

They were awkward and ignorant, yearning and desperate. Wilder sought power, and Bergman feared to lose it, and the others likely ran the same range of pleasant and obnoxious company that I remembered from my lost childhood congregation. But whatever else they might be, Spector had been wrong. The government had no more to fear from them than it had from Innsmouth eighteen years ago.

As Charlie shuts the door to the back room, I can see his hands trembling. Outside this room he wears a cynical elder's mask, but in truth he is in his late thirties—close enough to my age to make little difference, were we both common mortals. And life has been kind to him. What I now offer has been his greatest frustration, and his eagerness is palpable.

As he moves to clear the floor, I hold up my hand. "Later, we'll try the Inner Sea again"—his unaccustomed smile blossoms—"but first I need to read you something. It may help you to better understand what you're seeing, when you look into your own blood."

What I seek can be found in at least three books on his shelf, but I take down the children's text, flipping carefully until I come to the well-remembered illustration: Earth and her moon, with thirteen forms arrayed around them. I trace the circle with one too-long finger.

"I told you that you can take or leave the gods, but the history is real. This is that history. We have evidence, and eyewitnesses, even for the parts that haven't happened yet. The Great Race of Yith travel through space and through time, and they are brutally honest with those who recognize them. The Litany of Earth was distilled over thousands of years of encounters: conversations that together have told us all the civilizations that came before the human one, and all the civilizations that will come after we're gone."

I wait, watching his face. He doesn't believe, but he's willing to listen. He lowers himself slowly into a chair, and rubs his knee absently.

I skip over the poetry of the original Enochian, but its prompting is sufficient to give me the English translation from memory.

"This is the litany of the peoples of Earth. Before the first, there was blackness, and there was fire. The Earth cooled and life arose, struggling against the unremembering emptiness.

"First were the five-winged eldermost of Earth, faces of the Yith. In the time of the elders, the archives came from the stars. The Yith raised up the Shoggoth to serve them in the archives, and the work of that aeon was to restore and order the archives on Earth.

"Second were the Shoggoth, who rebelled against their makers. The Yith fled forward, and the Earth belonged to the Shoggoth for an aeon."

The words come easily, the familiar verses echoing back through my own short life. In times of hardship or joy, when a child sickened or a fisherman drowned too young for metamorphosis, at the new year and every solstice, the Litany gave us comfort and humility. The people of the air, our priest said, phrased its message more briefly: *This too shall pass.*

"Sixth are humans, the wildest of races, who share the world in three parts. The people of the rock, the K'n-yan, build first and most beautifully, but grow cruel and frightened and become the Mad Ones Under the Earth. The people of the air spread far and breed freely, and build the foundation for those who will supplant them. The people of the water are born in shadow on the land, but what they make beneath the waves will live in glory till the dying sun burns away their last shelter.

"Seventh will be the Ck'chk'ck, born from the least infestation of the houses of man, faces of the Yith." Here, at last, I see Charlie inhale sharply. "The work of that aeon will be to read the Earth's memories, to analyze and annotate, and to make poetry of the Yith's own understanding."

On I count, through races of artists and warriors and lovers and barbarians. Each gets a few sentences for all their thousands or millions of years. Each paragraph must obscure uncountable lives like mine, like Charlie's... like my mother's.

"Thirteenth will be the Evening People. The Yith will walk openly among them, raising them from their race's infancy with the best knowledge of all peoples. The work of that aeon will be copying the archives, stone to stone, and building the ships that will carry the archives, and the Evening, to distant stars. After they leave, the Earth will burn and the sun fade to ashes.

"After the last race leaves, there will be fire and unremembering emptiness. Where the stories of Earth will survive, none have told us."

We sit for a minute in silence.

"You ever meet one of these Yith?" Charlie asks at last. He speaks urgently, braced against the answer. Everything else I've told him, he's *wanted* to believe.

"I never have," I say. "But my mother did, when she was a girl. She was out playing in the swamp, and he was catching mosquitoes. Normally you find them in libraries, or talking to scholars, but she isn't the only person to encounter one taking samples of one sort or another. She asked him if mosquitoes would ever be people, and he told her a story about some Ck'chk'ck general, she thought the equivalent of Alexander the Great. She said that everyone asked her so many questions when she got home that she couldn't remember the details properly afterward." I shrug. "This goes with the magic, Mr. Day. Take them both, or turn your back."

✳

The basement door creaked, and skirts whispered against the frame.

"Oz," came Bergman's voice. "I wanted to talk to you about... Ah. It's you." She completed her regal descent. "Oz, what is *she* doing here?"

I rose, matching her hard stare. If I was to learn—or perhaps even teach—anything here, I needed to put a stop to this. And I still had to play a role.

"What exactly is it that you hold against me? I've come here many times, now. The others can see easily enough—none of them doubt what I am."

She looked down at me. "You could be an imposter, I suppose. It would be easy enough. But it's hardly the only possible threat we should be concerned about. If you are truly of the Deep Ones' blood, why are you not with your noble kin? Why celebrate the rites here, among ordinary humans who want your secrets for themselves?"

Why are you not with your kin? I swallowed bitter answers. "My loneliness is no concern of yours."

"I think it is." She turned to Wilder, who had kept his place before the altar. "If she's *not* a charlatan... either she's a spy, sent to keep us from learning her people's powers, or she's in exile for crimes we cannot begin to imagine."

I hissed, and unthinkingly thrust myself into her space, breathing the stink of her sharply exhaled breath. "They. Are. Dead."

Bergman stepped back, pupils wide, breath coming too quickly. She drew herself up, straightened her skirts, and snorted. "Perhaps you are a charlatan after all. Everyone knows the Deep Ones cannot die."

Again without thinking, I lunged for her. She stumbled backward and I caught her collar, twisted, and pulled. She fell forward, and I held her weight easily as she scrabbled to push me away. I blinked (eyes too big, too tight in their sockets), anger almost washed away by surprise. It was the first time the strength had come upon me.

And I had used it on an old mortal woman whose only crimes were pride and suspicion. I released her and turned my back. The joints of my fingers ached where I had clenched them. "Never say that again. Or if you must, say it to the soldiers who shot my father. We do not age, no—not like you do." I could not resist the barb. "But there are many ways to die."

Oz finally spoke, and I turned to see him helping Bergman to her feet. "Peace, Mildred. She's no spy, and I think no criminal. She will not take your immortality from you."

I paused, anger not entirely overwhelmed, and searched her features carefully. She was slender, small-eyed, fine-fingered—and unquestionably aged. For all her dignity, it was impossible that she might share even a drop of blood with my family.

She caught my look and smiled. "Yes, we have that secret from the Deep Ones. Does it surprise you?"

"Exceedingly. I was not aware that there *was* a secret. Not one that could be shared, at least."

A broader, angrier smile. "Yes—you have tried to keep it from us. To keep us small and weak and dying. But we have it—and at the harvest moon, I will go into the water. I am beloved of the Elder Gods, and I will dwell in glory with Them under the waves forever."

"I see." I turned to Wilder. "Have you done this before?"

He nodded. "Mildred will be the third."

"Such a wonderful promise. Why don't you walk into the ocean yourself?"

"Oh, I shall—when I have trained a successor who can carry on in my place." And he looked at me with such confidence that I realized whom he must have chosen for that role.

Mildred Bergman—convinced that life could be hoarded like a fortune—would never believe me if I simply *told* her the truth. I held up my hand to forestall anything else the priest might have to say. "Wilder, get out of here. I'll speak with you later."

He went. If he had convinced himself I would be his priestess, I suppose he had to treat me as one.

I sat down, cross-legged, trying to clear the hissing tension that had grown between us. After a moment she also sat, cautiously and with wincing stiffness.

"I'm sorry," I said. "It doesn't work like that. We go into the water, and live long there, because we have the blood of the deep in us. The love of the gods is not so powerful. I wish I had more to offer you. There are magics that can heal, that can ease the pains of age, that can even extend life for a few decades. I will gladly teach them to you." And I would, too. She had been vile to me, but I could invite her to Charlie's back room to study with us, and learn the arts that would give her both time and acceptance. All but one spell, that I would not teach, and did not plan to ever learn.

"You're lying." Her voice was calm and even.

"I'm not. You're going to drown yourself—" I swallowed. "I'm trying to save your life. You haven't done a speck of real magic in this room, you don't know what it's like, how it's different."

She started to say something, and I raised a hand. "No. I know you won't listen to what I have to say. Please, let me show you."

"Show me." Not a demand—only an echo, full of doubt.

"Magic." I looked at her, with my bulging eyes and thick bones, willing her, if she couldn't yet believe, at least to look at me.

"What's involved in this... demonstration?" she finally asked, and I released a held breath.

"Not much. Chalk, a pair of bowls, and a drop of blood."

Between my purse and the altar, we managed to procure what was needed—fortunate, as I would have hated to go up and ask Wilder to borrow them. Having practiced this with Charlie, I still had the most basic of seals settled in my mind, at least clearly enough for this simple spell. I moved us away from the carefully laid tile to the raw flagstone behind the stairs. There was no reason to vandalize Wilder's stage.

Bergman did not know the Litany, nor the cosmic humility that was the core of Sharlhyda practice. And yet, in some ways, she was easier to work with than Charlie. I could tell her to feel her blood as a river, without worrying what she might guess of my nature.

As I guided her through the opening meditation, Bergman's expression relaxed into something calmer, more introspective. She had some potential for the art, I thought. More than Wilder, certainly, who was so focused on the theater of the thing, and on the idea of power. Bergman's shoulders loosened, and her breath evened, but she kept her eyes open, waiting.

I pricked my finger and let the blood fall into the bowl, holding myself back from the spell long enough to wipe the blade and pass it to Bergman. Then I let the current pull me down...

Submerging only briefly before forcing myself upward, out of the cool ocean and into the harsh dry air. I took a painful breath, and laid my hand on Bergman's arm.

A thin stream moved through a great ravine, slow and emaciated. Rivulets trickled past great sandy patches. And yet, where they ran, they ran sweet and cool. The lines they etched, the bars and branches, made a fine and delicate pattern. In it I saw not only the inevitable decay that she strove against, but the stronger shape that was once hers—and the subtler strength in the shape she wore now.

"You *are* one of them."

I returned, gasping, all my instincts clamoring for moisture. I wanted to race upstairs and throw the windows open to the evening fog. Instead I leaned forward.

"Then you must also see—"

She sniffed, half a laugh. "I see that at least some of the books Wilder found can be trusted. And none of them have claimed that the Deep Ones are a more honest race than we. They do claim that you know more of the ancient lore than most humans have access to. So no, I don't believe that your immortality is a mere accident of birth. It can be ours as well—if we don't let you frighten us away from it."

We argued long and late, and still I could not move her. That night I argued with myself, sleepless, over whether it was my place to do more.

Of course Charlie asks, inevitably.

I have been teaching him the first, simplest healing spells. Even a mortal, familiar with his own blood, can heal small wounds, speed the passage of trivial illnesses and slow the terrible ones.

"How long can I live, if I practice this?" He looks at me thoughtfully.

"Longer. Perhaps an extra decade or three. Our natures catch up with us all, in the end." I cringe inwardly, imagining his resentment if he knew. And I am beginning to see that he must know, eventually, if I continue with these lessons.

"Except for the Yith?"

"Yes." I hesitate. Even were I ready to share my nature, this would be an unpleasant conversation, full of temptation and old shame.

"What the Yith do... there *are* spells for that, or something similar. No one else has ever found the trick of moving through time, but to take a young body for your own... You would not find it in any of these books, but it wouldn't be hard to track down. I haven't, and I won't. It's not difficult, from what I've heard, just wrong."

Charlie swallows and looks away. I let him think about it a moment.

"We forgive the Yith for what they do, though they leave whole races abandoned around fading stars. Because their presence means that Earth is remembered, and our memory and our stories will last for as long as they can find younger stars and younger bodies to carry them to. They're as selfish as an old scholar wanting eighty more years to study and love and breathe the air. But we honor the Yith for sacrificing billions, and track down and destroy those who steal one life to preserve themselves."

He narrows his eyes. "That's very... practical of you."

I nod, but look away. "Yes. We say that they do more to hold back darkness and chaos than any other race, and it is worth the cost. And of course, we know that we aren't the ones to pay it."

"I wonder if the... what were they called, the Ck'chk'ck... had a Nuremberg."

I start to say that it's not the same—the Yith hate nobody, torture nothing. But I cannot find it in me to claim it makes a difference. Oblivion, after all, is oblivion, however it is forced on you.

The day after my fourth meeting with Spector, I did not go to work. I walked, in the rain and the chill, in the open air, until my feet hurt, and then I kept walking, because I could. And eventually, because I could, I went home.

Mama Rei was mending, Kevin on the floor playing with fabric scraps. The *Chronicle* lay open on the table to page seven, where a single column reported the previous night's police raid on a few wealthy homes. No reason was given for the arrests, but I knew that if I read down far enough, there would be some tittering implication of debauchery. Mama Rei smiled at me sadly, and flicked her needle through a stocking. The seam would not look new, but would last a little longer with her careful stitching.

"You told him," she said. "And he listened."

"He promised me there would be no camps." Aloud, now, it sounded like a slender promise by which to decide a woman's fate.

Flick. "Does he seem like an honorable man?"

"I don't know. I think so. He says that the ones they can't just let go, they'll send to a sanitarium." Someplace clean, where their needs would be attended to, and where they would be well fed. "He says Wilder really does belong there. He believed what he was telling the others. What he was telling Bergman."

And she believed what he told her—but that faith would not have been enough to save her.

No one's faith ever was.

Flick. Flick. The needle did a little dance down and around, tying off one of her perfect tiny knots. Little copper scissors, a gift purchased with my earnings and Anna's, cut the dangling thread. "You should check on her."

"I don't think she'll want to see me."

Mama Rei looked at me. "Aphra-chan."

I ducked my head. "You're right. I'll make sure they're treating her well."

But they would, I knew. She would be confined in the best rooms and gardens that her money could pay for, all her physical needs attended to. Kind men would try to talk her back from the precipice where I had found her. And they would keep her from drowning herself until her blood, like that of all mortals, ran dry.

I wondered if, as she neared the end, she would still pray.

If she did, I would pray with her. If it was good for nothing else, at least the effort would be real.

The WICKED
SHALL COME UPON HIM

Kristi DeMeester

Twain met the girl on a night without stars. In the months leading up to her, darkness bled from the edges of the heavens, blotting out what had once glowed with quiet, white light.

Before the sky swallowed itself, the moon bloated, heavy and full. Later, it turned a rancid yellow, and people closed their doors and curtains to avoid the moonlight.

It took two weeks for that light to leak into people's skins and turn it the color of something spoiled, something rotted. An effect of the environment, the news said, and night after night, people drowned themselves in booze and pills in the hopes that they could ignore the screams pouring from the blackened sky.

People talked in low voices to each other and to themselves. Tried to dismiss their jaundiced skins as a temporary effect of the moon's shift, to brush off the screams as a seismic event. Every day another set of scientists on the television explained that eventually the moon would resume its natural cycle, but each morning, nothing had changed. The sun rose and shone without warmth. The night kept coming, and shadow spread like a blanket over the world.

Outside, under the darkness, people set fire to what they could find. Tore apart furniture. Couches and dining tables piled in front of their homes and set aflame. The darkness held at bay with weak, flickering light.

They fucked and sweated and pissed in the dirt. Hunted needles and injected confusion and chaos into their veins. A never-ending orgy at the end of the world. Like rats, they found themselves outside, where they sought the light of the many fires.

This is where Twain saw the girl. Outside of the apartment building in the courtyard he came to sometimes smoke, her lanky body crouched before a tree, long dark hair twisted into dreadlocks tipped with blue. He watched her peel apples with a razor blade. Long strips fluttered and twisted underneath her hands as the edge bit against white flesh.

"You one of Nathan's?" the girl asked him.

He didn't like the easy nature of Nathan's name in her mouth. Didn't like the way she assumed that he was just another fuck. *One of Nathan's.* The tone of her voice implying that he was nothing. He stroked the platinum band on his left hand, his fingers tracing the metal that covered the date inscribed beneath.

"We were married. Once," he said. "Before."

She nodded. "And now?"

"He wanted to throw a party. Outside. For the last time. Before whatever the fuck's going to happen happens."

The words were dead shells of what he wanted to speak. He'd learned to swallow the sharp teeth of his love, and the silence he carried within him was the only thing that kept him from grasping the girl's razor and drawing it across his throat.

"How do you know Nathan?" he said.

"He's easy to know. Everyone knows him," she said.

She was right. It was why he had fallen in love with Nathan when he was nothing more than a child. A seventeen-year-old high school dropout in the big city. He'd haunted the bars, giving the bouncers blowjobs in trash-filled back alleys to get in. The knees of his jeans absorbing liquid runoff from the garbage bins and rats bumping against his shoes as he stared into the distance, tried not to focus on the sweating, heaving body in front of him.

He'd met Nathan at Mary's on karaoke night, had watched him onstage growling out Tom Waits to a crowd screaming for him to take his fucking shirt off already.

Four bourbon waters later, he approached Nathan and screamed over the pumping music that Tom Waits sucked ass. To which Nathan laughed, called him a baby, and bought him another drink.

When the bar closed, Nathan pushed him into a cab, and they clawed at one another the entire twenty minutes to Nathan's apartment. In the living room, Twain learned the movements of Nathan's body, the taste of his sweat. He held it under his tongue, marveled at how love can blossom, hard and violent, like thorns shooting into the heart. Later, they spooned, Nathan's pale skin standing in stark contrast with Twain's dark.

Twain fell in love with him that first night. Three weeks later, they stood before a Justice of the Peace, and Nathan swore to love him until their bodies crumbled into dust.

"I'm Audrey," the girl said, and Twain started. He had forgotten her presence there, and she smiled up at him, her lips pressed in a tight line.

He opened his mouth to speak, but a quick movement to the left drew his attention. Two nude forms tumbled out of the dark, their skins sallow and streaked in dirt. Nathan and a man Twain didn't recognize. Their arms draped over each other and the man whispered into Nathan's ear. His breath would be hot, thick with whisky or wine, and Nathan would suck the words from his lips as if he were drawing the very essence out of him.

Twain swallowed. Watched the sky for something other than darkness, but there was nothing to see. Above them, the screams sounded again, a discordant melody of pain or hunger. Twain was afraid to know which.

When it had all began, Nathan disappeared for hours at a time. Came home reeking of smoke and liquor. Two weeks later, Nathan stumbled into the apartment and told him, "Why not have a good time while we can? Fuck who we want. Do what we want. Everything's going to shit, Twain. Can't we just *live*? For once in our lives, let's just forget the rules and do what we want."

"Fuck you, Nathan. If you bring anyone in here, into our *home*, I swear to Christ I'll fucking kill him," he'd said. He'd wanted to hit him.

Wanted to feel Nathan's blood under his fingernails and to know that it belonged to *him*. This blood was his alone, and he would tear apart anything that tried to take it from him. He would die before that happened.

The next week, their sheets reeked with another man's smell. All of the rage he'd felt the moment Nathan had told him what he planned to do melted away into a sobbing desperation.

He locked himself in the bathroom and swallowed the first bottle of pills he could find. Aspirin, it turned out. He thought his stomach had turned inside out, and he'd shit his pants, but his heart kept pounding in his chest. Nathan had not been there to hold it in.

Despite everything, he couldn't bring himself to leave.

"If I carve your name into one of these, you'll fall in love with me." Audrey twitched the razor toward the apples under her boots, and grinned. Her teeth were stained red.

"Wine?"

"What's that?"

"Red wine. Bitch of a stain."

"Should I do it? Should I cut your life into mine, Twain? Make you forget him? Forget the sound of your name in his mouth; the weight of his hand against your chest? All of your learned routines. Gone. Poof. Like smoke. You would be happy again."

Somewhere in the dark, Nathan laughed. Twain could no longer tell the sound from the screaming.

"How much more? How much more do I have to feel before there's nothing left?" he asked. Audrey shrugged her shoulders.

There was too much space in this new world the darkness had created. The fire casting a scant glow, and all of the shadowed things that lived beyond the haloed light stretching toward them, mouths gaping and hungry. Too many empty places where silence echoed through the words Nathan spoke.

Every day, other people drew their yellowed skins around them and cocooned the soft, fragile bits. All so they wouldn't see, wouldn't expose their raw, bleeding hearts. So they could ignore the empty sky and the possibility of whatever came next.

He could have done the same. He had tried. But Nathan would touch him, would tousle his hair, and he found himself confused and suffocating in what had been their love.

Audrey picked up another apple, traced the blade over the surface, her fingers appearing to shimmer. The blue fire of stars under her fingernails. He blinked, and the light vanished. She dipped into the apple. Began to carve.

"Why do you think it screams? The sky?" she said.

"I don't know."

"They're waking up. The old ones. That sound. It's the sound of the entire world opening."

Her words woke something inside of him, and his stomach twisted into knots. Strange to be frightened of the words spoken by a girl he didn't even know, but the fear grew all the same.

"What are you?"

"Something that has always been," she said.

"Twain! Come the fuck on already. Everybody's waiting." Nathan's voice seemed to come from everywhere at once. He thought the sound would tear him open. He couldn't breathe. The sky bore down, and the screams pitched ever higher.

"Everything devours itself. Lust. Hate. Love. We burn and burn until there is only ash, and then we eat what remains. Carry it inside of us like a secret. Until it grows into something else." Audrey brought an apple to her lips, bit down. Red teeth. White flesh.

He shuddered. Turned in the direction of Nathan's voice. He would take one of Nathan's pills. Chase it with whisky or vodka or absinthe. Forget the girl and the sky and her strange speech, her old ones coming awake. Forget the cold fear that had crawled up his spine when she spoke. Forget Nathan sweating and grunting against someone else. Forget the way Nathan had looked at him the day they met.

"So easy to do. To slip your fingers under the skin of love. Tug until it drops away. Show everything that lives underneath. All the broken little things," Audrey said, and took up another apple. Her wrist flicked. A small movement, and he felt himself tipping forward. An abyss yawning before him.

"The old ones will rise. Will give us new eyes. New mouths. Aren't you hungry, Twain? Don't you want to eat and drink of them and forget everything that came before?"

To forget. To have never known Nathan. To have his memory erased. To forget the pain of Nathan laughing, his head leaned against another man's chest. Forget.

"What happens if I say yes?" he asked her, and she stood—she was taller than he'd imagined—and pressed her lips to his. Her tongue was sweet, and he gagged.

Still, he opened his mouth wider to accept what she gave him. He closed his eyes, and dark stars blazed behind his lids. The moon glowed crimson. She poured the sky's screams into him—all of that ancient darkness—and the sound burned. Burned away everything. Bright and clean.

He didn't know when the girl pulled away, only that she had gone, the apples piled beneath his feet, her taste still in his mouth. The fire that Nathan had started had gone out, and the darkness licked at him. Filled him to the brim. He took off his shirt, his pants.

"Twain! What the fuck are you doing out there?" Nathan's voice floated from the entrance to the apartment building at his back.

He shouldn't still know that this was Nathan's voice, should he? He shouldn't feel the sudden need to move toward the sound, his feet finding their way back, his heart quickening. The girl—Audrey—had promised.

They lived on the ground floor of an apartment building that had been mostly abandoned. Vast rooms that carried only the ghosts of those who had once lived there. Family portraits still hanging in entryways; a pair of green rain boots left outside the door of 1406; an empty crib pushed against a bare window, a ragged stuffed elephant still inside.

He'd seen people packing, seen them loading cars with boxes or trash bags stuffed with clothing, but he could not remember their faces. These people who shared his walls had become nothing more than a wisp of memory.

Those who remained drifted in and out. Vague, amorphous shapes that he avoided when he encountered them in the lobby or the hallways, head down, eyes averted. If the others did the same, he didn't know.

He walked into the apartment now and found Nathan in the center of five men. All blonde. Smooth. Hairless. So much the opposite of Twain with his dark skin and dark eyes and thick hair that covered his arms and chest. So much the thing Nathan never claimed to want.

The entryway was lined with cheap Fuseli prints and opened to the living room with a tiny kitchen to the right. The refrigerator stood open, and bottles lined the countertop where a lone candle sputtered and cast shadowed devils against the ceiling. The air was stale and laced with the acrid smell of something faintly chemical.

The fake leather couch and cheap, flimsy end tables had been pushed against the walls of the living room to create open floor space. Nathan had taken their sheets and pillows, draped and piled them into some kind of obscene fort where these men Twain did not know wrapped muscled arms around each other.

Nested in a mound of blankets, Nathan reached for him. His pupils were too large, a deep black threatening to drown the sclera. The other men reached for him, too. A knotted tangle of limbs and fingers grasping at his naked legs, his bare belly.

"I've been waiting forever," Nathan said. *Forever.* The word hit him with the force of a bullet.

"I can't. We can't," Twain said, but Nathan tossed his hair and laughed. Twain's head swam, and the candle flame jumped, divided into two, then four, then hundreds of candles burning.

From the corner of the room, Audrey came crawling, her mouth drawn away from her teeth. The gums had gone black, and Twain's gorge rose in the back of his throat at the sight. He swallowed. Took a deep breath.

"Nathan. Please," he said, and the girl wrapped himself around his legs, her fingers burning against his calf.

"Jesus, Twain. Lighten up. Always so fucking intense. Have a drink. Or, if you're feeling frisky, Tyler here has something that will blow your goddamn mind."

"Please," he whispered, but Nathan drew him down among them. Hungry mouths sought out the soft, exposed parts of him. The taste of apples lingered on his tongue as he pushed them away.

Inside of him, the darkness moved, and he pictured tearing out the throats of the men with his bare hands, their yellowed skin withering beneath his touch.

If Audrey was still there, he could not find her among the mass of moving flesh.

Flashes of light blinded him. Nathan laughing. Nathan sleeping, his hands tucked beneath him like a child. Nathan holding him as he sobbed on the day his mother died.

He wondered if what the girl had given him would leak out of him, dribble from his lips like poison. If it was even possible for his bones to hold so much darkness. A pain so much like love. Everything and nothing all at once.

When he opened his mouth, the sky resumed its screaming. Whatever lived there, whatever dark angel or ancient god, shrieked, and the darkness stole into the room. The entryway, the bottles, the kitchen, fading into a blackened nothing. The men shrieked and clutched at one another, scrambled backward, but there was nowhere to go.

One by one, the other men were swallowed in shadow until only Twain and Nathan remained. And Audrey. She crouched beside them, her tongue darting over her lips.

Wherever the others had gone, Twain hoped their skins would be peeled from muscle, their tongues torn from their mouths. Hoped their blood would feed the sky, pour into the moon's ancient craters and carve strange sanguine rivers on the surface. And the old ones would drink and be satisfied.

"Twain. Oh, God. Oh, *God*. It's happening, isn't it? It's fucking happening. Oh, Jesus."

"What's left now, Nathan? Here at the end. What's left?"

"Jesus. Oh, Jesus. Fuck." Nathan's eyes were wild, beads of sweat appearing on his upper lip, his forehead.

"Why wasn't it enough? Why wasn't *I* enough? We could have gone into the dark together. One body. One flesh."

Twain could smell Nathan's fear, could feel the rapid beating of his heart quivering in the air. How much he wanted to take that delicate beating in his palm, cup it inside his hands to keep it safe.

"I've carried you inside of me. No matter how I try to starve you out, forget that you were ever there, you won't *leave*. I never wanted anything else, Nathan. There was never anything else."

The darkness hovered over them, waiting. The black just barely touching their legs, reaching for the brother that had curled inside of Twain. Soon, it would cover everything. They would never leave this place.

"I can't feel my feet, Twain. What the fuck? I can't feel anything."

"It should be so much easier now. She promised, but you're still inside of me. Still burning," he said. He wanted to cry, but there were no tears left.

Nathan wrapped his arms around him, and Twain leaned into the man he loved, breathed in the smell of his skin, the feeling of his hands against his neck.

Around them, the sky gaped open, the darkness enveloping everything.

"Yes," he whispered to the dark. He pressed his mouth to Nathan's, breathed into him.

And together, they waited.

AFTER RANDOLPH CARTER

Noah Wareness

1.

THE WAY THROUGH DEATH IS LOCATED in death, just as the way through the sky is located in the sky.

Those who train in lucid dreaming make it their reflex throughout the waking day to ask whether all phenomena are dreams: recalling this question during sleep brings liberation. As long as you are alive, you should ask if you are dead.

If you would turn back the world's patterns on themselves, rejecting the world, you would train for the way through death.

The way through death is felt as wonder.

2.

Blank-featured, wind-cloaked, the traveler from Providence glances away from the great silver key on its opal throne. There is a cord of some crystal filament, silver too, but not bright; it grows from inside his wrist and reaches all the way back to the world. This he wraps twice around his palm, as though to secure himself. Not taut, never quite touching the floor of the empty hall, it spills a blood-tincted shadow across the gray obsidian tiling. It is wider far than the cord, this shadow, and a metallic and liquescent quality marks it, as though blood were turning inside a vein of mercury. Where footfalls lately touched the ground, the shadow ripples metallically with their imprint. This hall belongs to a great king, it is said; or the silver key is somehow the bodily remains of the king, or the locus of his sovereignty. None have called it his manuscript, but the austere handwriting of Randolph Carter seethes blackly across the key from bow to tip. And all this is remarkable. The traveler clenches the long tether in his fist. Once beyond the gates, one ought to find no single thing remarkable over others.

3.

When beholding any phenomena, whether remarkable or mundane, ask if you are dead.

When you pour out water and eddies emerge in the stream, a miniature river with boiling, diaphanous banks, ask if you are dead.

When planes of warm sunlight slant through the leaded window, when they lie alongside your body as their meaningless geometry decomposes into noise, ask if you are dead.

When putting away the coming week's clothes and the late evening moon seems immeasurably near, ask if you are dead.

When walking, you gash your hand meaning to break a twig from a hedge; when looking back, many hands are hung from the hedge's thorns, trailing silver tangles of root from their ripped stumps, ask if you are dead.

When you regard a mirror, when it folds and divides like paper, becoming a sheaf of folded mirrors joined at the hinge with signatures of fraying mirror-twine, when mirrors reflect featurelessness, ask if you are dead.

When recopying the draft of a poem and the heel of your hand slips over the drying ink, blotting your skin with diffuse silver pictographs, ask if you are dead.

When stacking flints alongside an abandoned road, when they become a gray and heatless fire that never crackles but makes the grinding sounds of stone on stone, ask if you are dead.

Ask if you feel wonder.

4.

The silhouettes of vanished footfalls echo ever harder in the shadow, expanding and intercrossing, breaking against each other. His astral tether is not matter and should not cast shade at all, and the traveler stumbles forward half a step. He crouches there, staring, palms flat to the ground while the shadow billows and whips. For all he knows these footprints are not his but the king's. When he looks back the silver key has become a hollow, slender cone of no clear purpose, carved of yellow petrified wood. There are different markings, roughly incised: a passage beginning *Blank-featured, wind-cloaked, the traveler.* It is not written here whether you are dead or dreaming, what you ask, only that your body dissolves from the center out as you read, like a bundle of scarves untying and rustling into intangibility. Certain of your most well-worn memories settle in the mind of Randolph Carter, sovereign of Ilek-Vad. A line of gabled rooftops reflecting sunlight like clouds of golden steam. The sour-sweet taste of juice held with cloves in a gourd, approximating moon-tree wine. The smells of boot polish and old wet brick. Numerous others.

5.

What is the expression of a life spent toward death, Providence?

A gift to those we have never met.

What is its redemption from waste?

You do not know me, Randolph Carter.

About the Authors

RHOADS BRAZOS hails from Colorado, where he lives with his wife and son. His morbid fascination with horror and weird fiction takes his writing down paths he's perhaps too willing to follow. Somehow, his work has seeped into this anthology and other unsuspecting venues, including: *The Best Horror of the Year Volume 7* (edited by Ellen Datlow); *Apex Magazine*; *Death's Realm* (Grey Matter Press); and *SQ Mag*. The first installment of his occult detective novella series, *The Ladies Bristol: The Devil's Trill*, is slated to be released by Grey Matter Press this summer.

KRISTI DeMEESTER writes spooky, pretty things in Atlanta, Georgia. Her work has appeared or is forthcoming in *Apex Magazine*, *The Dark*, Year's Best Weird Fiction Volumes 1 and 3, and others. Her chapbook *Split Tongues* was published by Dim Shores Press in early 2016.

STEFANIE ELRICK is an artist, performer and word weaver from England. Originally from the windswept moors of Yorkshire she was wooed by Manchester's industrial charm (and rave scene) and began her path in theatre and dance. After a decade of creating fantasy stage shows for the likes of Hawkwind, and various other misfits, she turned to performance art and rekindled a love affair with literature. In collaboration with Loren Fetterman she's blood-lined poetry onto her body during a live event *Written in Skin* and been strapped to a spinning timepiece for four hours throughout *KAIROS*. She's fascinated by shape-shifters, magic and rites of passage and can never resist the call of the Black Gnosis. www.stefanieelrick.com

RUTHANNA EMRYS lives in a mysterious manor house in the outskirts of Washington DC with her wife and their large, strange family. She makes home-made vanilla, obsesses about game design, gives unsolicited advice, occasionally attempts to save the world, and blogs sporadically at ashnistrike.livejournal.com and on Twitter as @r_emrys. Her stories have appeared at Tor.com, *Strange Horizons*, and *Analog*. Her first novel, *Winter Tide*, will be available from MacMillan's Tor.com imprint in April 2017.

JOHN LINWOOD GRANT lives in Yorkshire with a pack of lurchers and a beard. He may also have a family. He has an obsession with Edwardian horror and alienation, but occasionally leaves his comfort zone for explorations of contemporary darkness. His most recent works range from madness in period Virginia to tales of the monsters we ourselves become. You can find him every week on greydogtales.com, often with his dogs.

VRAI KAISER is a writer, essayist, and somewhat alarming Herbert West enthusiast. They're a regular contributor to *The Mary Sue*, and their stories appear in Torquere's *I Do* anthology and *Rock and Roll Saved My Soul*. You can read more fiction and essays at vraikaiser.com or tweet @writervrai

JAMIE MASON is a Canadian author of dark SFF whose most recent novels are *Kezzie of Babylon* and *The Book of Ashes* (Permuted Press). His short fiction has appeared in *On Spec, Abyss & Apex* and the *Canadian Science Fiction Review*, among other places. He lives on Vancouver Island. Learn more at jamiescribbles.com

LUKE R. J. MAYNARD is a writer, poet, musician, and literary critic from London, Ontario, Canada. He completed his PhD in English at the University of Victoria in 2013. His work has appeared in anthologies and journals across Canada and the United States—including in the 2014 Martian Migraine Press anthology *Conqueror Womb*.

KONSTANTINE PARADIAS is a writer by choice. His short stories have been published in the *AE Canadian Science Fiction Review*, Atelier Press' *Trident Magazine* and the *BATTLE ROYALE Slambook* by Haikasoru. His short story, *How You Ruined Everything* has been included in the Tangent Online 2013 recommended SF reading list and his short story *The Grim* has been nominated for a Pushcart Prize.

DON RAYMOND lives in the tiny hamlet of Alturas, CA, where he works as an accountant at the local casino, which is not a career path his counselors had ever mentioned to him. He spends his free time mediating the Machiavellian feline politics of his household. You can read more of his work at *The Saturday Evening Post* and *Everyday Fiction*, or find him online at cthulhuconspiracy.wordpress.com. He also once didn't make a left turn at Albuquerque.

ERICA RUPPERT writes speculative fiction and poetry from her home in northern New Jersey. Her work has appeared in *Nonbinary Review*, *Eternal Haunted Summer*, *Weirdbook*, and Robot Cowgirl Press's *Alien Abduction* anthology. You can find her on Facebook and Twitter and at nerdgoblin.com

JAYAPRAKASH SATYAMURTHY lives in Bangalore, India with his wife Yasmine, several dogs, even more cats and a bass guitar. Owls sometimes drop by. His chapbook, *Weird Tales Of A Bangalorean* was published in 2014 and he has a second chapbook, *A Volume Of Sleep*, due sometime in 2016.

Like so many before him, **GORD SELLAR** was introduced to the work of H.P. Lovecraft by a stoner/geek co-worker at a music store in Edmonton. Though mainly an SF author, he's made a sideline in weird fiction, with Lovecraftian stories appearing in *Clarkesworld*, *The Book of Cthulhu II*, and *Cthulhu Fhtagn!* He also screenwrote and composed the score for South Korea's first Lovecraft screen adaptation (the award-winning *The Music of Jo Hyeja*). Aside from a few years spent investigating the shadowy horrors of Saigon, he's lived in South Korea continually since 2002. Among his many ongoing writing projects is a collection of short stories mashing together Korean history and Lovecraftian cosmic horror. Drop by gordsellar.com if you feel like it.

NOAH WARENESS lives with some friends in the city. He writes by hand. You can read his work at noahwareness.tumblr.com

BRYAN THAO WORRA is an award-winning Lao-American writer. An NEA Fellow in literature, he is a member of the Horror Writers Association and the Science Fiction Poetry Association. His work appears internationally, including *Innsmouth Free Press*, *Tales of the Unanticipated*, *Astropoetica*, *Outsiders Within*, *Dark Wisdom*, and *Mad Poets of Terra*. He is the author of several books of speculative poetry: *On the Other Side of the Eye*, *BARROW*, and the award-winning *DEMONSTRA*. Visit him online at thaoworra.blogspot.com

About the Editor

SCOTT R JONES is a writer, spoken word performer, mostly unintentional comedian, and naturalized sorcerer. He lives in Victoria BC Canada with his lovely wife Sasha and all-round awesome kids Sean and Meridian. His fiction and poetry has been published in *Broken City Mag, Innsmouth Magazine, Cthulhu Haiku 2, Andromeda Spaceways Inflight Magazine,* and a few anthologies and podcasts besides. His book detailing an auto-ethnographical approach to religious themes and practice derived from Lovecraft's Cthulhu Mythos, *When The Stars Are Right: Towards An Authentic R'lyehian Spirituality,* has received praise from the likes of Laird Barron, Ross E. Lockhart, and Richard Gavin, and apparently caused S. T. Joshi to make a squicky face when it was mentioned during a convention panel. You can reach him by email at srjones@martianmigrainepress.com or you can follow him on the Twitter @PimpMyShoggoth

Be sure to check out these other Martian Migraine Press titles…

WHEN THE STARS ARE RIGHT:
Towards An Authentic R'lyehian Spirituality
by Scott R Jones

PRIESTESS
the collected BLACKSTONE Erotic Series, Volume One
by Justine Geoffrey

RESONATOR: New Lovecraftian Tales From Beyond
edited by Scott R Jones

martianmigrainepress.com

Follow us on Twitter @MartianMigraine

Lightning Source UK Ltd.
Milton Keynes UK
UKHW020729041121
393378UK00010B/261